Truthful Jane

Florence Morse Kingsley

Alpha Editions

This edition published in 2024

ISBN : 9789362512994

Design and Setting By
Alpha Editions
www.alphaedis.com
Email - info@alphaedis.com

As per information held with us this book is in Public Domain.
This book is a reproduction of an important historical work. Alpha Editions uses the best technology to reproduce historical work in the same manner it was first published to preserve its original nature. Any marks or number seen are left intentionally to preserve its true form.

Contents

CHAPTER I .... - 1 -
CHAPTER II .... - 7 -
CHAPTER III .... - 12 -
CHAPTER IV .... - 19 -
CHAPTER V .... - 29 -
CHAPTER VI .... - 38 -
CHAPTER VII .... - 46 -
CHAPTER VIII .... - 54 -
CHAPTER IX .... - 60 -
CHAPTER X .... - 66 -
CHAPTER XI .... - 73 -
CHAPTER XII .... - 80 -
CHAPTER XIII .... - 85 -
CHAPTER XIV .... - 90 -
CHAPTER XV .... - 96 -
CHAPTER XVI .... - 101 -
CHAPTER XVII .... - 108 -
CHAPTER XVIII .... - 113 -
CHAPTER XIX .... - 121 -
CHAPTER XX .... - 128 -
CHAPTER XXI .... - 134 -

CHAPTER I

Miss Jane Evelyn Aubrey-Blythe stared steadily at the toes of her damp, shabby little boots which peeped out from beneath the hem of an equally damp and shabby gown, her youthful brows puckered thoughtfully over a pair of extraordinarily bright, long-lashed hazel eyes. Miss Blythe, was for the moment, feeling very much out of it, and consequently very unhappy.

The room in which she was sitting, drying her damp boots and petticoats by a smoldering fire of logs, was a sufficiently cheerful one, its two large windows commanding a wide view of red-tiled London roofs and glazed chimney-pots, all of which glistened wetly in the dull light of the late afternoon. For the rest, the red Turkey carpet was badly worn in spots; the chairs presented the appearance of veterans staunchly surviving a long and stormy career; while the two small desks piled with dog-eared school-books exhibited tokens of strenuous usage in the shape of ineradicable ink-stains, which served to diversify the cuttings and carvings of inexpert jackknives, stealthily applied.

At opposite sides of a table in the center of the room two small boys in knickerbockers were actively engaged in a competition in which large china mugs of milk and water, and thick slices of bread and butter and jam figured conspicuously.

"You'd better come to your tea, Jane, before we eat all the bread and butter," advised one of the boys thickly.

"I don't want any tea, Cecil; and you shouldn't talk with your mouth full; it's very rude," replied the girl tartly.

"You'll get no dinner, you know, because there's company," observed the other boy, slamming his mug on the table. "Old Gwendolen won't have you down because you're so much handsomer than she is."

Jane turned a distractingly pretty profile toward the speaker, a slight smile dimpling the corners of her mouth. "You oughtn't to say such things, Percy," murmured the girl "—though I dare say it's true enough," she added plaintively.

The two boys, having variously disposed of the thick slices of bread and butter, were now causing startling explosions to issue from the depths of their mugs.

"Put down your mugs this instant!" ordered Miss Blythe sternly. "Haven't I forbidden you to make those disgusting noises in your milk?"

"You have—yes," admitted Cecil coolly, as he sent his empty mug spinning across the table; "but who cares for you, anyway! You're only a poor relation!"

With a smothered howl of rage the smaller Percy arose from his place and fell upon his brother, who received the attack with practiced courage, while Miss Blythe resumed her moody contemplation of her steaming boots.

"You're a cad!"

"You lie!"

"You're another!"

"Ouch!"

"Leggo!—Leggo, I say!"

The tugging and panting of the small combatants, and the scuffling of their stout little shoes on the threadbare carpet, quite drowned the slight sound of the opening door.

"Cecil—Percy—*my sons*!" exclaimed a voice.

Jane Blythe shrugged her slim shoulders wearily in anticipation of what was to follow.

"I am surprised and displeased, Jane, that you should permit such a disgraceful scene to take place in the school-room without even attempting to quell it," went on the lady, advancing majestically into the center of the floor. "What do I see?—bread and butter on the *floor*, on the *sofa*, on the— yes, actually, *on the mantle!* and *milk*— Really, Jane, I fear you sadly forget your duties at times."

Miss Blythe had risen, apparently that she might bring her bright hazel eyes more nearly on a level with the frozen blue ones behind the double glasses which pinched the lady's aquiline nose.

"I don't forget my duties, Aunt Agatha," she said distinctly; "but I think you have forgotten to pay me for them."

"What do you mean, ungrateful girl?"

"I mean that if I am to perform the duties of a nursery governess in your house I should be paid regular wages the same as the rest of the servants. My shoes are worn through the soles, and I need—everything. Even Parks dresses better than I do. She can afford to."

A dead silence followed this clear statement of fact. The two small boys were sulkily regarding their mother from beneath their light lashes, who, in her turn, attempted to quell the militant light in the eyes of the girl.

"How—*dare* you say such a thing to me!" cried the lady at length. "And before the children, too! You may come to me in the library to-morrow morning, Jane, when I am examining the accounts. I will talk with you then. In the meantime"—Lady Agatha Aubrey-Blythe paused to draw her rustling gown more closely about her tall figure—"I would advise you to reflect on the fact that when you were entirely alone in the world, *helpless* and *penniless*, I took you into my house and cared for you like—like——"

Jane Blythe laughed aloud. It was a dreary little sound; somehow it caused Percy to clench his small fist and draw a little nearer to his cousin.

But it appeared to enrage the lady. Her patrician countenance assumed a peculiar, sickly, mottled pink colour. "To-morrow, at ten, in the library," she said coldly. "And, Jane, as Parks will be occupied with my toilet, I should like you to assist Gwendolen. You may go down now. Susan will put this disgracefully untidy room to rights. Cecil and Percy, you will go to bed at once—*at once!* do you hear?"

"Yes, mother," piped the two small scions of the house of Aubrey-Blythe in a respectfully subdued chorus. After which they proceeded to thrust their agile tongues into their red cheeks and bulge out their round, blue eyes behind their maternal relative's august back as she turned to leave the room.

"You'll catch it to-morrow, Miss Jane—at ten—in the library!" opined Master Cecil sagely. "I'll bet she'll smack you with the ruler."

"Hold your tongue, Cecil, and come on to bed!" bawled Percy, "or you'll be the one to get smacked with the ruler."

Miss Blythe had walked over to the window and was looking out with unseeing eyes into the gathering dusk.

"It is true," she told herself forlornly. "I am poorer than any of the maids in the house. I hate it! Oh, how I *hate it all*!" She wiped away two or three rebellious tears on a grimy little pocket-handkerchief.

A servant had entered and was somewhat noisily gathering the empty dishes onto a tray. "I see you've 'ad no tea, miss," she observed kindly. "Shan't I toast you a bit o' bread at the fire an' fetch some more jam?"

"No, Susan, thank you; I must go down now. But you're very kind to have thought of it."

Jane's smile was beautiful, and the warm-hearted Susan, for one, appreciated it. "They'd orto to be 'shamed o' theirsel's," she observed vaguely to the tea things, as the girl closed the door softly behind her. "An' she's pretty's a pink, an' that sweet-mannered! She'd orto marry a r'yal dook, that she 'ad; an' dress in di'mon's an' satings!"

Susan was in the habit of solacing herself with yellow-covered romances in the scant leisure stolen from her duties as housemaid, and of late Miss Jane Evelyn had figured as the heroine of everyone of these tales in the honest damsel's rather crude imaginings.

As Miss Blythe passed down the dimly lighted staircase on her way to her cousin's room, she was startled to the point of uttering a slight scream by a dark figure which darted out upon her from behind a tall suit of armor stationed on the landing.

"O Reginald!" she exclaimed, "why will you play such baby tricks, now that you are nearly grown?"

"'Nearly grown,' indeed!" echoed the tall youth in a displeased voice. "I am grown. Look at me—away over your head, Miss Jane! I say, give us a kiss, will you?"

"No, indeed, I'll not! Get out of my way directly. I'm in a hurry!"

"Oh, no, you've lots of time to talk to me," chuckled Reginald, planting his ungainly figure directly across the stair. "And you'll not go a step farther till you've paid toll. Do you know, Jane, you're growing deucedly pretty—upon my word!"

"Impudence!" cried Jane sharply. "If you don't let me go this instant I'll call your mother."

"If you do that," drawled the boy, wagging his head threateningly, "I'll tell the mater you were trying to kiss me. Then you'd catch it; she'd believe me every trip."

By way of reply to this taunt Miss Blythe reached up and dealt the tall youth a stinging slap on his beardless cheek.

"Tell her that a girl cuffed you, too, baby!" she retorted, and slipped past him like a shadow.

"I'll pay you out for that, miss! See if I don't!" threatened Reginald. But Jane was safely out of sight and hearing, too.

The tall girl seated before a dressing table, carefully inspecting a rather rough and muddy complexion by the light of two wax candles, turned frowning eyes upon Jane as she entered the room.

"Where have you been keeping yourself, slow-poke?" she inquired crossly. "Don't you know I'll be late if I don't make haste?"

"You'd better make haste then," advised Jane coolly, advancing with her hands behind her back. Her usually pale cheeks were flushed to a lovely pink by her triumphant escape from Reginald; her brown hair, ruffled into crisp waves, fell about her brilliant eyes. "What do you want me to do, Gwen—hook up your frock?" she added carelessly.

"I want you to dress my feet first, and be quick about it, too," replied Miss Gwendolen haughtily. "No; not those pink stockings!— I've decided to wear all white this evening. The open-work silk ones, stupid! What is the matter with you, anyway, Jane? You're as red as a lobster."

Jane's little hands trembled as she pulled the designated hose from a pile of party-colored ones in the tumbled drawer. "Here are your stockings," she said briefly. "Which shoes do you want?"

"The white suede with straps; they're the freshest—and do make haste!" replied Gwendolen impatiently.

Jane set the large, white, high-heeled shoes down on the floor beside her cousin's chair with a loud thump.

"Well, aren't you ever going to put them on?" demanded Miss Gwendolen, kicking her satin bedroom slippers half across the room.

"No; I'm not. You can put them on yourself," said Jane deliberately. "Why should I put on your shoes and stockings for you, Gwendolen? You never put on mine for me—do you?"

Gwendolen stared at Jane's rebellious face in silence. She was a dull girl, and it took her some time to understand what Jane had really said to her.

"Why, why—" she stammered, "you have always done as you were told before, and—I'll tell mother," she added, an ugly frown distorting her face. "She'll not allow you to be impertinent to me, you know."

"It is quite impossible for me to be impertinent to you, Gwendolen," said Jane, drawing up her little figure superbly. "One cannot be impertinent to one's equals. I'll hook up your frock for you, if you like, because you are my cousin, and I ought on that account to be willing to be civil to you. But I won't put on your stockings and shoes for you, so you may as well begin."

Gwendolen stooped and drew on her stockings in sullen silence; then she put on her shoes. "I'll tell mother," she repeated stupidly.

"You may tell her if you like," said Jane airily. "And you may tell Lady Maybury that you haven't sense enough to pull on your stockings straight, if you like. I don't care."

Gwendolen looked actually frightened; she peered into her cousin's face with her ugly, shortsighted eyes. "What *has* come over you, Jane?" she asked anxiously. "Oh, I do believe you've got a fever and are out of your head! Get away from me—do! Suppose it should be smallpox, and I should catch it—oh! Go away—quick! Ring the bell for Susan as you go out. She can hook my frock, and——"

Jane pirouetted out of the door like a sprite. "Thank you, Gwen!" she cried mockingly. "Yes, I fancy I have a fever. But you'll not catch it, you poor, dear, stupid thing, you!"

Then she darted up two flights of stairs to her own cold little room under the roof, where she flung herself face downward across the narrow bed and wept tempestuously.

"O God, *please* let me go away from this house!" she prayed between her sobs. "I've been good and patient just as long as I possibly can. Things will *have* to change!"

The girl was truthful—even with herself—even with her Creator.

CHAPTER II

Jane Aubrey-Blythe was not in the habit of weakly shedding tears; nevertheless on this occasion she wept herself into a state of somnolence like a whipped child, when she lay quite still, her handkerchief rolled into a tight, damp ball, her limp figure shaken with an occasional recurrent sob.

"They are all too hateful," she murmured brokenly. "I wish something would happen—anything; I don't care what."

As a matter of fact, something did happen almost immediately. As Jane was sleepily pulling the blankets about her chilly shoulders, Susan's honest face, shining like a hard red apple in the light of the candle she carried, was thrust inside the door.

"O Miss Jane Evelyn," she whispered, "are you 'ere?"

"What is it, Susan?" demanded Jane, sitting up and winking drowsily at the candle flame.

"W'y, you've 'ad no dinner, miss, an' so I've brought you a bite of chicken and a mouthful of salad," said Susan briskly. "Just you lie back comfortable-like on these 'ere pillows, miss, an' I'll bring it in directly."

"But I'm not ill, Susan, and I'm not hungry," protested Jane. "I—I'm just tired."

"You'll be ill directly if you don't pick a bit o' somethink," Susan declared oracularly, "an' you that slender an' delicate, Miss Jane Evelyn." She was arranging the contents of a neat tray before Jane as she spoke. "Now you jus' try a mossel o' that bird, an' you'll find it tastes moreish, or I'm mistook i' the looks o' it. Miss Gwendolen, now, is that thick i' the waist she might go wi'out her dinner for a fortnight, that she might, miss. It was all I could do a-'ookin' up 'er frock this very evenin'. 'You're such a stoopid, Susan,' she says, 'your fingers is all thumbs.' Then she turns an' twists afore 'er glass as proud as proud, though the Lord knows she's nothink to be proud of, wi' that rough, muddy skin o' hers, alongside of yours, Miss Jane Evelyn."

"You are very impertinent, Susan," said Jane reprovingly. "Gwen can't help her complexion, nor her thick figure, though of course they must get on her nerves, poor thing." And Jane dimpled demurely, as she tasted her salad with appetite. "I was hungry, after all," she acknowledged.

Susan gazed at the young lady with admiring eyes. "Of course you were, Miss Jane Evelyn," she exulted, "an' I knowed it. As I says to cook, 'Miss Jane Evelyn's 'ad nary bite o' supper,' I says; an' cook says to me, 'Susan,' she says, 'you'll find a tray i' th' buttry, once I'm through wi' dishin' up.'"

Jane's eyes filled with fresh tears; and she choked a little over her tea. "You're too good, Susan," she murmured, "and so is cook, to think of me at all."

"All I hasks in return, miss, is that you'll take me on as lidy's maid once you're married an' settled in a 'ome o' your own."

Jane fixed wistful eyes upon Susan's broad, kindly face. "O Susan," she said, "do you suppose I'll ever have a home of my own?"

"Do I suppose you'll ever— W'y, land o' love, Miss Jane Evelyn, in course you will! Mussy me, don't I *know*? Ain't I seen young ladies in my time? There was Miss Constance and Mary Selwyn, both of 'em thought to be beauties, an' me scullery maid an' seein' 'em constant goin' in an' out of their kerridge through the area windy, where I was put to clean vegetables; an' they wasn't a patch on you, miss, fer figure, nor yet fer complexion, nor yet fer eyes, nor yet——"

"O Susan!" exclaimed Jane soulfully, "you oughtn't to talk that way. I'm not at all pretty."

"You're jus' beautiful, Miss Jane Evelyn," said Susan firmly, "beautiful enough fer a dook or a prince, if it's only me as says it; an' you'll see what you'll see some o' these days, that you will. W'y, only last night I was tellin' your fortin' wi' cards, miss, an' the dark man wi' a crown was fightin' a dool wi' the light man, an' all for the love of you, miss; an' if that ain't a sign o' somethin' serious then I don't know cards nor fortins neither."

"That will do, Susan," said Jane, very dignified indeed. "Thank you so much for bringing me something to eat, and will you thank cook for me, too. I think I will go to bed now, Susan, and you may take the tray away."

"I'll take the tray down directly, Miss Jane Evelyn," said honest Susan, quite unabashed, "but go to bed you'll not, miss, because the master wishes to see you quite pertic'lar in the library when 'e's through 'is dinner."

"What! Uncle Robert?" exclaimed Jane, flying out of bed, and beginning to pull the pins out of her tumbled hair. "I wonder what he can possibly want with me." Her little hands trembled. "Oh, I'm afraid Aunt Agatha——!"

"No; it ain't, miss," beamed Susan encouragingly. "I'll bet it's somethink himportant, that I do. I was jus' a-comin' downstairs after Miss Gwendolen's flowers, an' the master was standin' in the 'all. 'Where's Jane?' he says to my Lidy. 'She should be down by this.' An' my Lidy she says, 'aughty an' cold-like, 'Jane 'ad her supper in the school-room with the children, as usual, to-night,' she says. 'She didn't care to come down.' 'Why, dang it,' 'e says, or some such word, 'Jane ought to be down to-night of all nights; 'aven't you told her, madam?' 'No,' says my Lidy, 'I 'aven't. I left that to you.' Then 'e turns to me, an' horders me to tell you to be in the library at ten o'clock, an' to say that you was to wait for 'im there till 'e come. It ain't much after nine, miss, so you've time a-plenty, an' I'll 'elp you to dress."

Jane's eyes were shining like frightened stars. "Oh!" she murmured brokenly, "I wonder what it can be!"

"Now, don't you be scared ner yet worrited, Miss Jane Evelyn," exhorted Susan, her head in Jane's little wardrobe. "You just put on this 'ere white frock an' I'll 'ook it up fer you. But first I'll do your 'air, if you'll let me."

Jane resigned herself with a sigh to Susan's deft hands. "You do brush my hair so nicely, Susan," she murmured, after a long silence filled with the steady stroking of the brush through her long brown tresses.

"It's the Lord's own mussy you'll let me do it, miss," cried Susan fervently, "else a 'ouse-maid I'd live an' die, an' me wantin' to be a lidy's maid sence I was knee high to a grass-'opper. I says to Miss Gwendolen on'y yesterday, 'Mayn't I brush your 'air, miss,' I says, 'Parks bein' busy, I think I can do it satisfactory.' 'Go 'way, Susan!' she snaps out, 'do you s'pose I'd 'ave your great, rough, clumsy 'ands about my 'ead?' she says."

"Your hands are not rough, nor clumsy, either," said Jane, understanding the pause, and filling it exactly as Susan wished; "and if I ever do have a lady's maid it shall be you, Susan."

"Thank you kindly, Miss Jane Evelyn," beamed Susan. "Now ain't that a lovely coffer? I'll bet Parks couldn't do no better nor that in a hundred years! But it 'ud be a simple idgit what couldn't do your 'air, miss; it's that soft an' shinin' an' curls itself better nor curlin'-tongs could do it."

All of which was strictly true, as Jane's brown eyes told her. Then the white frock was carefully put on, and Susan next produced from somewhere three great creamy buds, one of which she fastened behind Miss Blythe's pretty pink ear; the other two she pinned to the modest little bodice, standing off to survey her handiwork with an air of honest pride.

"I 'ooked them three roses from Miss Gwendolen's bouquet," she announced unblushingly, "an' a mighty good job it were."

"Then I'll not wear them," said Jane decidedly. "You may take them away, Susan. I may be forced to wear Gwen's cast-off frocks; but I'll *not* wear her flowers!"

An ethical differentiation which it would have puzzled Miss Blythe to explain, and which left poor Susan in open-mouthed dismay.

"She's a reg'lar lidy, is Miss Jane Evelyn, as ever was," cogitated that worthy hand-maiden, as Jane's light step passed down the corridor, "'igh an' 'aughty as the 'aughtiest, yet that sweet an' lovely in her w'ys I can't 'elp a-worshipin' the ground she walks on. It's a dook or a lord as ought to marry Miss Jane Evelyn, an' it's me as 'll be her lidy's maid." And she proceeded to put the poor little room with its shabby appointments into truly exquisite order with all the zeal born of her anticipations.

There was no one in the library when Jane entered it, so she sat down in one of the great carved chairs by the fire, feeling very small and young and lonely. The gentle hum of conversation and the subdued tinkle of glass and silver reached her where she sat, and between curtained doorways she could catch glimpses of the softly lighted drawing-room beyond, gay with masses of azaleas and ferns.

After a little Jane found herself busy with dim memories of her past. She had been a child of three when her father and mother died, within a month of each other, she had been told; the broken-hearted young wife apparently not caring enough for her one child to face her bleak future.

"Oliver Aubrey-Blythe's wife was an exceedingly weak woman," Lady Agatha had once told Jane cruelly; "and I feel that it is my duty to train *you* into something far different, if such a thing is at all possible."

Jane's little hands grew quite cold, as she strove vainly to fix the illusive memory of the two faces which had bent over her on the day she had fallen into the fountain at Blythe Court. She remembered the fountain distinctly, with its darting goldfish and the stout cherub in the middle staggering under the weight of an impossible dolphin from whose open mouth gushed a dazzling jet of water.

There were blue flowers growing about the edge of the marble basin, and she had recklessly trampled them under foot in her baby efforts to grasp a particularly beautiful goldfish. The rest was a blur, wherein dazzling blue sky seen through green waving treetops an immense distance away made a background for the two shadowy figures which stood out from the others. It was pleasant at the bottom of the fountain, Jane remembered, where one could look up through the clear water and see the far blue sky and the waving trees. For an instant she paused to wonder what would have happened had the shadowy figures of her parents been farther away when she shrieked and fell—quite at the other side of the garden, say. Would the blue sky and the waving trees have faded quite away into nothingness after a little? And was somethingness so much better than nothingness, after all?

But all this ghostly cogitation being quite at variance with Miss Blythe's usual optimistic and cheerfully human way of looking at things, she presently abandoned it altogether to speculate on the nature of the interview with her uncle, an event which certainly concerned her immediate fortunes much more intimately. Mr. Robert Aubrey-Blythe was an exalted personage with whom Jane felt herself to be very slightly acquainted. He was kind; yes, certainly. Jane could not recall a single occasion upon which he had spoken to her in a manner even remotely approaching unkindness. Indeed, he very rarely spoke to her at all beyond a curt 'Good evening, Jane' when she slipped into her place at the family dinner table. Twice before this she had been summoned to the library; each time to receive a perfunctory rebuke for some childish piece of mischief, reported presumably by Lady Agatha; whereat she had gone away shaking in her small shoes to lead a blameless existence for many days thereafter.

"Aunt Agatha has told Uncle Robert what I said to her about being paid for teaching Percy and Cecil," the girl decided. "Well, I hope she has. I don't mind being a nursery governess, not in the least; but I hate—hate—*hate* the way I am living now. Even the servants pity me!"

She stood up and drew her slight figure to its full height as she heard the swish and rustle of silken skirts in the corridor; the women were coming away from table. It was a small party, after all. Jane watched the vanishing trains of the five dinner-gowns with a speculative smile. How would it seem, she wondered, to be beautifully dressed every night and dine with guests who were not forever carping at one, but whose chief business in life it was to be agreeable. Then she faced about at sound of her cousin Gwendolen's voice.

"What are you doing in here, Jane?" demanded that young lady snappishly, as she advanced to the fire.

"Waiting for Uncle Robert," Jane told her briefly.

Gwendolen frowned and twisted her rings so as to make them sparkle in the firelight. "How *very* coy and unconscious we are!" she said sneeringly. Then suddenly she burst into a disagreeable laugh.

"What are you laughing at, Gwen?" asked Jane, with real curiosity.

"At you, goose," replied Miss Aubrey-Blythe crossly. She turned and moved toward the door. "Don't you know what papa wants with you?" she paused to demand.

"No, I don't," said Jane steadily. "Do you?"

But Miss Gwendolen merely shrugged her ugly shoulders as she dropped the heavy curtains into place behind her.

CHAPTER III

When Mr. Robert Aubrey-Blythe finally entered the library, it was with the pleasant glow of a good dinner, good wine, and good company enveloping his portly form like a visible halo. He actually bowed before Jane, as though she were a great lady of his acquaintance, instead of his niece, left on his hands to bring up with scarce a penny to her name.

"Ah, Jane," he began, swelling out the shining expanse of his shirt front like a pouter pigeon, "I see—er—that you are here, as I bade you."

"Yes, Uncle Robert," murmured Jane, with a beating heart; "you wished to speak with me, sir?"

"I did, Jane; I did indeed. Ah—er—you may be seated, if you please, Jane."

Jane obeyed.

"Why—er—did you not come down to dinner to-night, Jane?" Mr. Aubrey-Blythe wanted to know next, his remark being prefaced by a long and speculative stare at Jane's small person. He appeared indeed to be looking at his niece for the first time.

"Because I wasn't asked, sir."

"Hum—ah; it was an oversight, Jane. You should have dined with us to-night."

Jane was puzzled. She stole a glance at her uncle's eminently respectable British visage, with just a fleeting wonder as to the amount of wine he had drunk at dinner. But no; he was undeniably sober, not to say serious; his eyes were still fixed upon herself with that singularly speculative gaze.

"You have—er—made your home with us for many years—that is to say, since your infancy, Jane, and I—er—trust that these have been not unhappy years—eh, Jane?"

Jane folded one cold little hand over the other; it was as she thought, she told herself angrily, Aunt Agatha had blabbed. "Since you have asked me, Uncle Robert," she said distinctly, "I will tell you that they have been very unhappy years. I simply hate my life in this house." She leaned back in her chair and fixed her clear eyes upon her uncle. Manifestly he was astounded by her reply.

"Why, why, why—upon my word!" he stammered at length. "I am—er—shocked to hear you speak in that manner. What—er—what, in short, do you mean?"

"I should rather go away and earn my living," said Jane desperately. "I suppose Aunt Agatha has told you what I said to her in the schoolroom to-night; but I meant it; I shouldn't mind being a nursery governess in the least, and"—forlornly—"it is all I am good for."

"Tut, tut!" remonstrated Mr. Aubrey-Blythe with some sternness. "You quite misunderstand me, I see. Now, I beg that you will have the goodness to attend me while I explain more fully why I have sent for you."

But he made no haste to enter upon the promised explanation, again fixing his eyes upon his niece in a long, contemplative gaze. What he saw must have clarified his ideas somewhat, for he presently went on more briskly.

"Whether you have been happy or not during your years of residence under my roof matters little with regard to—er—what I am about to say, Jane. I have, in short, a proposal for your hand."

"A what?" gasped Jane.

"A proposal of marriage was what I said," repeated Mr. Aubrey-Blythe rebukingly. "A most honorable and—er—highly flattering proposal, in short. I own that I was surprised, and so—er—was my wife, Lady Agatha."

Jane's own emotions were clearly depicted upon her young face. She was leaning forward in her chair, her large eyes fixed upon her uncle.

"Who—" she began; then stopped short.

"You have, of course, met the gentleman who has paid you this great compliment—the highest compliment—er—that man can pay to woman," proceeded Mr. Aubrey-Blythe grandly. "The proposal reached me by letter last week, and the author of that letter was"—he paused dramatically—"the Hon. Wipplinger Towle."

The girl burst into a hysterical laugh.

"Jane, I beg— Will you not control yourself, madam? Ah—er—I see I shall be forced to call Lady Agatha."

Jane instantly became calm. "Don't—please don't call Aunt Agatha," she begged. "It was only—I couldn't help thinking——"

"I trust you will reflect carefully as to what this proposal means for you, Jane. I confess that I should have been—er—not displeased had the proposal embraced a different—that is to say—er—had the recipient of it been my own daughter, I should have been disposed to consider it not unfavorably. Lady Agatha was at first convinced that the gentleman had, in short, committed a most egregious blunder; but I am assured by word of mouth that this is not the case. It is you, Jane, he wishes to make his wife; you and no other. And I congratulate you sincerely upon the auspicious event. I will not deny that your future has been an occasional source of keen anxiety to me, and also, I believe, to my wife, Lady Agatha; portionless brides are not commonly sought by men—er—whose position in life is that of the Hon. Wipplinger Towle."

"But—Uncle Robert; you can't mean that I— You know I—couldn't *marry* that man, Uncle Robert."

"You could not marry the Hon. Wipplinger Towle? Surely, I do not understand you correctly, Jane. I perceive that you have been greatly surprised by the nature of my disclosure, totally unprepared for it as you were. And this much I regret, my dear child. You should have been apprised of the facts, you should indeed."

Jane's heart was touched by the faint cadence of affection in the man's voice. "O Uncle Robert!" she cried, "do you look at all like my father? Do tell me that you do; I should so love to think so!"

Mr. Aubrey-Blythe shook his head. "I do not resemble my deceased brother Oliver in the smallest particular," he said dryly. "And I have never felt that this was a cause of regret. Oliver was a most injudicious and hasty tempered person; his early death and many misfortunes were undoubtedly brought about by his own deplorable imprudence. I have often thought"—deliberately—"that you resemble him, Jane."

"I'm glad I do!" retorted Jane. "And I may as well say once for all, Uncle Robert, that I will *not* marry the Hon. Wipplinger Towle. You may tell him so."

Mr. Robert Aubrey-Blythe regarded his niece with a portentous gathering of his bushy eyebrows. "I beg, Jane," he said, "that you will not decide this matter hastily. There are, in short, many reasons why you should marry, and I will not deny that I regard the present proposal as most opportune. I have, in short, given the Hon. Wipplinger Towle my full permission to pay his addresses to you. He dined with us this evening, and—er—expects, I believe, the opportunity of pleading his own cause."

"Do you want me to go away, Uncle Robert?" faltered Jane, quite overcome. "Do you hate me, too?"

"Certainly not—decidedly not, Jane. You—er—put the matter in most unwarranted terms. But I believe that you would be far happier in an establishment of your own. In fact, you have already intimated something of the sort in the course of our conversation. Am I not right?"

"I said I should rather be a nursery governess," said Jane doggedly. "I can do that; I have taught Percy and Cecil ever since Miss Craddock went away, and——"

Mr. Robert Aubrey-Blythe rose abruptly. "No, Jane—I beg— Keep your seat, if you please. I will send Mr. Towle to you at once. You are, of course, at liberty to do as you wish in the matter. But as your eldest surviving male relative I most strongly advise that you listen to his suit patiently and give him the answer that he wishes and—er—expects."

Jane stretched out her hands imploringly. "Dear Uncle Robert," she whispered; "please, Uncle Robert—just a minute!"

But he was gone, and Jane sank back in her chair with a sob. "Oh, if he would only love me a little!" she thought. Then she sat up very straight and calm; somebody was approaching.

The Hon. Wipplinger Towle was a tall man, even taller than Mr. Robert Aubrey-Blythe. He was also exceedingly lean, and bald—quite bald. Jane mechanically noted the dull pale glisten of his scalp as he crossed the wide expanse of Turkey carpet which intervened between herself and the curtained doorway.

"Good evening, Mr. Towle," she said calmly, offering the tips of her chilly little fingers with extreme nonchalance.

The Honorable Wipplinger was evidently somewhat agitated in a perfunctory, elderly way. That he was likewise perfectly confident as to the outcome of the interview Jane thought she perceived, with an involuntary deepening of the dimple at the corner of her mouth.

"Hum—ah," he began, fixing his glass firmly in place. "You were not dining at home this evening, Miss Blythe? I was—er—frightfully disappointed, upon my word; I had been—ah—led to expect—ah—that is, I hoped that I should see you earlier in the evening."

"I never come down when Aunt Agatha has guests," said Jane, putting her pretty head on one side and gazing at her elderly suitor contemplatively. He was quite as old as Uncle Robert, she decided, and sufficiently ugly to look at, with his bald head and his tall, square-shouldered figure. For the rest, the Hon. Wipplinger Towle was possessed of a stubborn-looking chin, deep-set gray eyes, and a well-cut mouth, amply furnished with strong white teeth.

Jane gently shrugged her shoulders as she dropped her bright eyes to her lap. "I fancy I should have starved if it hadn't been for Susan," she finished.

Mr. Towle glanced at her quickly. "Hum—ah, Susan?" he hesitated; "and who, if I may ask, is Susan?"

"Susan is the under housemaid," replied Jane sweetly. "She brought me up some supper on a tray. Wasn't it nice of her?"

Mr. Towle made several small uncertain sounds in his throat, which resembled—Jane reflected—the noises made by an ancient clock on the point of striking. Then he stared hard at Jane, again adjusting his monocle. "Hum—ah, Miss Blythe," he began, "I—er—in point of fact, I have the very great honor to be permitted to pay you my addresses, and so——"

Jane turned pale. "Please don't mention it," she interrupted.

"I beg your pardon," observed Mr. Towle interrogatively, "you were saying———"

"I said, please don't talk about it. I—I couldn't, you know; though I'm sure it's very kind—at least, Uncle Robert said it was— A compliment, I believe he called it."

"One I am—er—delighted to pay to so lovely a creature as yourself," murmured Mr. Towle laboriously.

"How *dare* you say such a silly thing to me!" snapped Jane, her hazel eyes blazing. "I'm not a lovely creature, and I won't be called so."

"Why—er—I beg your pardon, I'm sure," stuttered the abashed suitor. "But I have the full permission of Lady Agatha and Mr. Aubrey-Blythe, and I thought— But surely you cannot have understood that I"—welling visibly with a sense of his own importance, Jane was resentfully sure—"desire to make you my wife. I wish you, in short, to make me the happiest man in London by—er—becoming Mrs. Towle. And may I, my dear Miss Aubrey-Blythe, beg you to name an early day—a very early day for the celebration of our nuptials. The matter of settlements and all that can be quickly arranged; and I beg to assure you that they shall be satisfactory—quite satisfactory, as I have already taken the pains to assure your uncle, Mr. Aubrey-Blythe. I can, in short, afford to be generous, and—er—I desire to be so."

Mr. Towle paused in his halting discourse to draw a small box from his waistcoat pocket. Jane watched him in fascinated silence as he opened it and drew from its satin nest a hoop of diamonds.

"I hope you will allow me," murmured the Honorable Wipplinger, bending forward.

"No!" cried Jane. "I say *no*!" She stood up, very pale and unapproachable. "I ought not to have allowed you to say all this to me," she said. "I do thank you for wanting me to marry you; but, of course, it is impossible."

"Why do you say 'of course'?" asked Mr. Towle, in a surprisingly human voice. "Do you enjoy your life here so much?"

"No," said Jane, "I do not; but I'll not marry to escape from it."

The Honorable Wipplinger deliberately returned the hoop of diamonds to its nest, snapped the lid of the box shut, and slipped it back into his waistcoat pocket. "I didn't go at it right," he observed meditatively. "Robert should have warned me." He turned to Jane once more. "Do you—er—mind telling me just why you have turned me down so squarely?"

"I'd much rather not," said Jane, blushing. "You wouldn't like it."

"Oh, yes, I should. For one thing, you think I'm horribly old; don't you?"

"Well, you are; aren't you?"

"Not so very. I lost my hair in a beastly fever I had in India ten years ago, and it would never grow on top after that. As a matter of fact I'm only forty."

"Forty!" repeated Jane, in an indescribable voice. "Why that—" She stopped short. "I'd much better say good night at once," she said contritely, "and—and truly I do thank you. I didn't suppose anyone in the world would ever care about me. And you———"

"I certainly do," said Mr. Towle resignedly. "But I went about saying it like a jackass. To tell you the honest truth I was in a regular blue funk. I never proposed marriage to a woman before, and I never shall again. Of course, you don't know me very well, Miss Blythe; but I'm a whole lot nicer than I look. If you only could———"

Jane shook her head decidedly. "I'd like you awfully well for—for an uncle," she said regretfully, "or a—grandfather— There! I oughtn't to have said that. You're really not old enough for a grandfather. But mine are both dead, and I've always thought it would be lovely to have one."

Mr. Towle swallowed hard. "Go on," he said encouragingly, "you'd like me well enough for a—a grandfather, but not for a husband. Is that what you meant to say?"

"It wasn't a bit nice of me to say it; but then I'm always saying dreadful things. That is why"—dejectedly—"nobody likes me."

The Hon. Wipplinger Towle gazed down at the little figure with a very kind look indeed in his deep-set gray eyes. "Oh, well," he said, "I might have known better. I did know better, in fact. But from something Lady Agatha said to me I fancied that perhaps I—that perhaps you———"

Jane held out her hand. "Good night," she said.

Mr. Towle took the offered hand in his very gently. It was cold, and the small fingers trembled a little in his own big, warm palm. "Good night," he said; "I can't—by force of cruel circumstances—be your—er—grandfather; but I'd like to be your friend, Jane; may I?"

"Why, yes," said Jane, smiling up into the keen gray eyes, "you may. And—and I thank you a whole lot for being so—game."

CHAPTER IV

Lady Agatha Aubrey-Blythe looked up from the housekeeper's book which she was inspecting with displeased interest, and turned her light blue eyes upon her husband's niece, as she stood a forlorn yet rigidly defiant little figure, her back against the closed door. "You may come in, Jane, and sit down," said Lady Agatha, in precisely the same tone she would have used to a delinquent housemaid.

Jane advanced and sat down, every line of her face and figure expressing an exasperating indifference to the stately hauteur of the lady, who on her part proceeded to concentrate her entire attention upon a bundle of tradesmen's accounts, which she compared one by one with the entries in the housekeeper's book.

This went on for some twenty minutes, during which period Jane stared unremittingly out of the window against which a cold rain was beating.

Then Lady Agatha spoke: "I have purposely detained you in complete silence, Jane, that you might reflect quietly upon your present position in life. I trust you have made good use of the opportunity."

Jane made no reply; but she withdrew her eyes from the dripping window pane and fixed them upon her aunt. In return, Lady Agatha focused her frozen stare upon the girl. "Is it *possible* that you had the *presumption* to refuse Mr. Towle's offer of marriage last night?" she asked with an indescribable mixture of unwilling respect and cold dislike in her voice.

"Yes, Aunt Agatha, I did," said Jane, a faint expression of regret passing over her face.

"Why?"

"Because I—couldn't—love him."

Lady Agatha scowled. "I *cannot* understand what attracted the man to you in the first place," she said disdainfully. "I believe he only saw you twice."

"Three times," Jane corrected her.

"You are not," said Lady Agatha, pausing to contemplate the girl's face and figure with the air of one examining a slightly damaged article of merchandise, "at all attractive. You have neither beauty nor style, and you are not in the least clever."

Jane appeared to grow smaller in her chair. She sighed deeply.

"Besides all this," went on Lady Agatha mercilessly, "you are practically penniless. I cannot understand how such a man as Mr. Towle, exceptionally well connected and very wealthy, *ever* came to think of such a thing as marrying *you*! But"—spitefully—"I dare say *you* know well enough how it came about."

"I don't know what you mean, Aunt Agatha," stammered poor Jane.

"Have you never met Mr. Towle, quite by accident, we will say, on the street, or——"

"How can you say such a thing to me, Aunt Agatha!" cried Jane, "as if I were a—servant, or a—a quite common person. I never saw Mr. Towle except in this house, and I never spoke three words to him before last night. And—and I do like him, because he—likes me. But I cannot marry him on that account."

Lady Agatha shrugged her shoulders with a hateful smile. "Oh, I dare say Mr. Towle will be very glad of the outcome later on," she said carelessly. "It is not easy to account for the vagaries of elderly men. But it was not to speak of this absurd *contretemps* that I sent for you this morning, Jane; Gwendolen reported to me what took place in her room last night, and at first I contemplated referring the whole matter to your uncle; but——"

Lady Agatha paused to note the gleam of hope which lighted up the girl's expressive features, only to fade as she went on in her peculiarly frigid, precise way:

"I finally thought best to settle the question with you. Your proposal that I should pay you the wages of a servant shocked and grieved me—*inexpressibly*. Your position in this household is that—er—of—a relative—an unfortunate relative, it is true; but still a relative. You bear our name, and as an Aubrey-Blythe you ought to consider what is due your—er—position. You ought, in short, to fill your humble niche in the family life cheerfully and uncomplainingly. Do you follow me?"

"Yes, Aunt Agatha," said Jane stonily.

"It is little indeed that you can do for us in return for all the benefits which are continually heaped upon you," went on Lady Agatha, with an air of Christian forbearance. "It ought not to be necessary for me to remind you of this, Jane. I regret that it is so. But I cannot permit a discordant element to disturb the peace of my home. You are aware that Percy and Cecil should be required to conduct themselves like gentlemen. You will see to it that the disgraceful scene of last night is not repeated. As for Gwendolen, any little service that you are requested to do for her ought to be gladly performed.

Do you know, the poor, dear child was quite overcome by your rudeness; she thought you must be ill."

"I shall never put on Gwendolen's stockings and shoes for her again," remarked Jane, with disconcerting finality.

"Jane, you forget yourself!"

"No, aunt; you are mistaken. I am not forgetting myself; I am remembering that I am an Aubrey-Blythe."

Lady Agatha stared blankly at the girl for a full minute. Then she recovered herself. "You are an ungrateful, impertinent girl!" she said slowly. "If you were younger I should feel it my duty to ferule you severely. There is one other thing I wish to speak to you about; then you may go. I have observed that you are far too familiar and presuming in your manner toward your cousin Reginald. His future position in the world as my oldest son and his father's heir does not warrant any such attitude on your part."

"Did Reginald tell you that he tried to kiss me on the stairs last night, and that I slapped him for it?" inquired Jane, in a businesslike tone. "It was 'familiar' of me, I admit; but Reginald is such a cub, you know."

Lady Agatha rose to her full height. "You may go to your room, Jane, and stay there for the remainder of the day," she said in an awful voice. "I see that my Christian charity is entirely misplaced in your case. I shall, after all, be obliged to consult your uncle with regard to some other disposal of your person. I cannot bear you about me longer. Your influence on my dear children is *most unfortunate!*"

Jane turned sharply—she already had her hand upon the door. "I hope uncle will send me away!" she exclaimed passionately. "I hate this house and everyone in it—except Percy and Susan!"

Lady Agatha, shaken out of her usual icy self-control, darted forward. She was a tall, big woman and she swept the girl before her in a blast of cold fury up the stairs—two flights of them—to the little attic room; there she thrust the slight figure within, and locked the door upon it.

Jane stood in the middle of the floor and listened to the ugly click of the key and the sound of Lady Agatha's retreating boot heels on the uncarpeted corridor.

"Well," said Jane ruefully. "I *have* made a mess of it!" She had completely forgotten her prayer of the night before.

Somebody had laid a fire in her rusty little grate. It was Susan, of course, who was continually going out of her way to be kind to the girl to whom everyone else was so persistently and pointedly unkind. Jane's sore heart warmed toward honest Susan, as she hunted for a match in the ugly little safe on the mantel. "I've a day off, anyway," she told herself, "and I'll cobble up that old gown of Gwen's so that I can wear it."

Miss Blythe was well used to cobbling up old gowns and clever at it, too. She waxed increasingly cheerful as she spread the faded breadths across her knee and discovered that the wrong side of the fabric was fresh and bright. Later she congratulated herself upon a stray sheet of *The Times*, left behind by Susan after laying the fire; it would do admirably for pattern material. As she spread its crumpled folds upon her counterpane, preparatory to evolving a wonderful yoke design, her eye fell upon a line in the column of "Female Help Wanted." It read as follows:

> "A lady about to travel in America wishes to engage intelligent young female as companion. Good wages. Duties nominal. Apply mornings to Mrs. Augustus Markle, 10 Belgravia Crescent."

"Oh!" murmured Jane Blythe. She sank down on the edge of her hard little bed and read the fateful lines again. "A lady about to travel in America—an intelligent young female as traveling companion. Why, *I* am an intelligent young female!" exclaimed Jane, with the air of a discoverer; "I wonder if I look the part?"

She stared at her young reflection in the dim mirror over her little dressing table. "I believe I look sufficiently 'intelligent' to perform 'nominal duties' as a companion," she told herself candidly. Then she hunted for the date of the paper, and was ready to shed tears of disappointment when she discovered that it was that of the previous day.

"There are so many intelligent young females, and I suppose everyone of them would like to travel in America," said Jane, still eying the brown-eyed young person in the glass. "Besides, I'm locked in."

The brown eyes twinkled as they turned toward the one window of the attic room. More than once, when she was a small girl, Jane had escaped from durance vile by way of the projecting gutter just outside her window. It was a perilous feat; but Jane was muscular and agile as a boy, and of a certain defiant courage withal, born perhaps of her unhappy lot in life.

"It would vex Aunt Agatha frightfully if I should fall and get killed on the conservatory roof," murmured Jane, as she pinned up her long skirts securely, "and it would cost Uncle Robert a whole lot in broken glass and potted plants and things; but I don't care!"

In another minute she had crawled out of her little window and commenced her dangerous journey to a neighboring window, which, luckily for the bold adventuress, stood wide open. Twice the girl's cautious feet slipped unsteadily on a bit of ice, and once the gutter itself cracked ominously under her weight; but at last she gained the window, climbed in, and sank white and shaken to the floor.

"Jane Blythe, you must be losing your nerve," she told herself sternly, when she had gathered sufficient strength to stumble dizzily to her feet; "the last time you tried that you didn't turn a hair!"

The rest was easy, and in less than an hour's time Miss Blythe found herself ringing the bell at 10 Belgravia Crescent. The slatternly maid, distinguished by the traditional smudge over one eye, informed her that Mrs. Markle was within, and in the same breath that she was "clean wore out with interviewin' young females."

Jane's heart sank; nevertheless she bestowed a sixpence upon the dingy maid with an air of regal unconcern, and was straightway ushered into the presence of Mrs. Augustus Markle, with a flourish of the dingy one's plaided pinafore and the brief announcement: "'Ere's another of 'em, ma'am!"

The stout lady, solidly enthroned upon a sofa before the dispirited fire, did not turn her elaborately coiffured head.

"Ze young woman may come in," intoned a full, rich, foreign-sounding voice which somewhat prepared Jane for the large, dark, highly colored visage, flanked with dubious diamond eardrops, which Mrs. Markle turned upon her visitor.

"You wis' to inquire about ze situation—eh?" pursued this individual, without any token of impatience. "I haf already seen feefty of ze London demoiselles *ce matin*."

"Oh, if you have already engaged some one, I will not trouble you!" stammered Jane, edging toward the door.

"Not so fast—not so fast, madmoiselle; it iss true I haf already engage; but—Ah, zis iss bettaire! More *chic*—*oui*. Your name, *s'il vous plaif*?"

"Jane Evelyn Aubrey-Blythe," murmured the girl.

"An' you wis' to go to ze ozzer side—to America—*oui*?"

"I wish to leave London; yes."

"To-morrow evenin', zen, I go by ze train. Zen I sail on ze so gra-a-nd ship. You go wiz me—eh?"

Jane stared at the woman with some astonishment. "What would be my—my duties?" she asked.

"Your duties? Why, to go wiz me—my *compagnon de voyage—comprenez*? Nossing else, I assure you; I wait on myself. But I am—what you call it—lone-some—see? An' I require a nize, young lady to go wiz me."

Mrs. Markle smiled affably, revealing a double row of glistening white teeth. She looked very kind and good-natured, and Jane drew a quick breath.

"I will go," she said decidedly.

The final arrangements were quickly concluded, and Jane presently found herself walking down the street, her cheeks flushed, her brown eyes blazing with excitement.

"I am going to America to-morrow—to-morrow!" she told herself. "I shall travel! I shall see the world! I shall never—never come back!"

The girl was so absorbed in her thoughts, which had for the moment flown quite across seas to the America of her imaginings, that she failed to see the tall, square-shouldered person who had turned the corner and was approaching her at a leisurely pace. She became aware of his presence when he spoke, and flushed an indignant scarlet as Lady Agatha's insinuating words recurred to her mind. "Yes," she returned vague answer to his greetings, "it is very pleasant to-day."

"But you," said Mr. Towle, smiling down at the little figure, "seem to be in great haste about something. You are quite out of breath. Suppose we go into this little park and sit down quietly and rest a bit. Your face is uncomfortably flushed."

"I can't help my color," murmured Jane confusedly; "it isn't because I was walking fast, but only——"

"Is it because you are vexed at seeing me?" Mr. Towle wanted to know. "We agreed to be friends last night, remember."

"I know it," said Jane, glancing up at him quickly. He looked much younger in his hat, she reflected, and he really had very nice eyes. "But I am going out of town directly," she made haste to add, "so we shall not see each other again—at least not for a long time."

"You are going away?" said Mr. Towle blankly. "Where—if I may ask without seeming impertinent?"

"I don't know exactly," replied Jane, with a provoking smile. "I am going to travel." Then she bit her tongue till it hurt. "Really, now you will see why I must hurry home at once. And—and, please don't mention what I have said to—to Aunt Agatha or Uncle Robert."

Mr. Towle regarded her in puzzled silence. "I beg your pardon," he said stiffly. "You were referring to what passed between us last night? I have already told your—ah—guardians the result of my proposals, and they——"

"Oh, I didn't mean that!" cried Jane. "How could you think so? I meant—Oh, *won't* you go away and not talk to me any more about it! You oughtn't to have liked me anyway. Aunt Agatha said so. She told me this morning that I was not at all attractive, and I am poor, too—perhaps you didn't know that—and—and—I am not at all clever; you can't help seeing that for yourself. I hope you will forget that you ever saw me those three times at Uncle Robert's."

"One time would have been enough for me," said Mr. Towle earnestly; "but as a matter of fact I have seen you more than three times. I never counted the occasions, but I saw you as often as possible, as for example when you went out with the two little boys in the governess cart, and when you walked with them in the Park, and twice in the Museum. Do you remember the day you showed them the mummies? You were telling them a long story about a little Egyptian princess; then you showed them the toys found in her tomb, and the mummy itself wrapped in browned linen, a withered lotus flower stuck in the bandages."

Jane stared at him meditatively. "I didn't see you anywhere about," she said.

"No; I took good care that you should not," Mr. Towle observed. "Now I am sorry for it."

"Why?" asked Jane; then bit her tongue again in her confusion. "I—I mean it would have been very—nice. I should have said I——"

"I was a bally idiot," pursued Mr. Towle steadily, "not to have taken the pains to become acquainted with you in any way, however unconventional. If I had, perhaps you would not have disliked me so."

"Oh, but I do not dislike you in the least!" protested Jane.

"If you could like me a very little," he said eagerly, "perhaps in time you could—Jane, if you are fond of travel I would take you all over the world. You should see everything. I thought I was done with happiness till I saw you. I had nothing to look forward to. I had seen everything, tested everything, and found everything empty and hateful, but with *you* at my side— Won't you try to like me, Jane?"

What Jane would have replied, had she not glanced up on the instant, she never afterwards felt entirely sure. But glance up she did to meet Gwendolen's scornful eyes fixed full upon her as she whirled past them in the Aubrey-Blythe victoria, with a great show of Aubrey-Blythe liveries on the box.

Instantly the forlorn little shoot of gratitude which was trying its feeble best to masquerade as sentiment in Jane's lonely heart withered and died under the icy blast of impotent anger and fear which passed over her. "She will tell Aunt Agatha," thought poor Jane, "and Aunt Agatha will think I have lied to her about seeing Mr. Towle on the street."

By some untoward psychological process, quite unperceived by herself, the full torrent of Miss Blythe's wrath was instantly turned upon the man at her side.

"I think I must say good morning, Mr. Towle," she said coldly. "I am really very much occupied to-day. I am sure I thank you for thinking of me so kindly—" She stopped determinedly and held out her hand.

And the Hon. Wipplinger Towle, feeling himself to be dismissed in all the harrowing length and breadth of the word, took his leave of her instantly, with a courteous lifting of his hat which afforded Jane a parting glimpse of his prematurely bald head.

"It must be dreadful to be bald," reflected Jane, with vague contrition, as she walked away; "but I can't help it." The correlation of these two ideas being more intimate and profound than appears in a cursory reading of them.

The door of Lady Agatha's morning room stood open as Jane attempted to slip past it like a guilty shadow. Gwendolen, still attired in her hat and jacket, evidently saw her and apprised her mother of the fact, for Lady Agatha's pursuing voice arrested the girl in full flight toward her own room.

"You will, perhaps, be good enough to inform me, Jane, how you came to be on the street after I had locked you into your own room for the day," intoned Lady Agatha, in a terrible voice. "*Deceitful, ungrateful, vulgar* girl, that you are!"

"I saw you, sly-boots; so you needn't deny it," put in Gwendolen, with a spiteful laugh. "It was passing strange how our demure Jane chanced to have a proposal, was it not? Do you know, mamma, Ethel Brantwood told me this morning that *that man* had been seen tagging Jane all over London. It is quite the common talk."

"Oh!" cried Jane, wringing her hands. "What *shall* I do?"

"Do not attempt to hoodwink me longer, unhappy girl," pursued Lady Agatha. "Your deceit, ingratitude, and *vulgar intrigues* are all laid bare. I have not decided what I shall do with you. It appears"—dramatically—"that locks and bars are no barriers to *you*. My commands you defy, my counsels you ignore, my affections you trample under foot!"

"Stop, Aunt Agatha!" cried Jane. "I did climb out of the window after you had locked me in—I wish now that I had fallen on the conservatory roof and killed myself; you wouldn't have minded anything but the broken glass—but you *must* believe that I never saw Mr. Towle on the street before. He *has* followed me about; he told me so this morning. But he never spoke to me once, and I did not know it. I never have thought of seeing him."

"How extremely ingenuous and naive!" put in Gwendolen, with an ugly titter; "quite after the pattern of a cheap variety actress, indeed! I wonder, mamma, that Mr. Towle took the pains to propose marriage to Jane in the dull, old-fashioned way. He might as well have eloped without ceremony."

Jane stared at her cousin, her face slowly whitening. "Do you realize what you have said to me, Gwendolen?" she asked in a stifled voice. "Yes. I see that you do. If you were a man I should—*kill* you. But you are only *you*, so I shall content myself by never speaking to you again."

"Gwendolen, my *love*, will you kindly leave us for a few minutes," said Lady Agatha, very calm and stately. "I cannot permit your young ears to be sullied by this mad talk. Really, I fear that the unfortunate girl's reason has been—" She paused significantly and touched her forehead. "I am told there has always been a marked weakness in her mother's family. Go, my love, go!"

"I shall go, too," said Jane bitterly. "I have nothing more to say to you, Aunt Agatha. I have told you the exact truth, and you may believe it or not as you like." She turned and followed Gwendolen out of the room.

That young lady, hearing the step behind her, fled with a hysterical shriek to the shelter of her mother's room. "What do you think, mamma, the creature was actually pursuing me!" Jane heard her say.

Then Jane went slowly up the stairs to her own room, where she remained quite alone and undisturbed for the remainder of the day. At intervals, during the course of the dreary afternoon, she could hear faint sounds of opening and shutting doors below stairs. Once Percy's loud voice and the clatter of his stout little shoes appeared to be approaching her room; then some one called him in a subdued voice; there was a short altercation carried on at a gradually increasing distance; then silence again.

A horrible sense of disgrace and isolation gradually descended upon the girl. She sobbed wildly as she looked over her few cherished possessions preparatory to packing them in the box she dragged in from the attic; her mother's watch, a locket containing her father's picture, a ring or two, her shabby little gowns and meager toilet things. By the time she had locked and strapped the box with shaking fingers she was shivering with cold and faint with hunger.

The latter primal urge finally drove her forth and down the rear stairways to the kitchen, where she found the servants in full tide of preparation for dinner.

"Lud ha' mussy, Miss Jane Evelyn!" cried Susan. "Where 'ave you be'n to look that white an' done hup?"

"In my room," said Jane shortly. "Will you give me some tea and bread, Susan? I'll take it up myself. No; please don't follow me. I wish to be alone."

"Somethink's hup wi' 'er," observed cook sagaciously, as Jane disappeared with a brace of thick sandwiches cut by the zealous Susan.

"They'd orto be 'shamed o' theirsels; that they 'ad, a-puttin' upon a sweet young lady like Miss Jane Evelyn," opined Susan. "I'd like to give 'em all a piece o' my mind; it 'ud do me good. It would so!"

"You're a goose, Susan," laughed cook. "An' so is she, if all I 'ear is c'rrect. Tummas says as 'ow that military-appearin' gent wot comes 'ere is crazy to marry 'er. An 'e's rich's cream!"

"Oh, lud!" sniffed Susan, her nose in the air, "'e may be rich, but 'e's bald as a happle! She'd never 'ave 'im; I'll bet me hown 'air an' me combin's to boot."

CHAPTER V

When Jane awoke the next morning she stared for a moment at the brownish spot in the ceiling just over her bed, as she had done every morning during a series of London seasons. It was a sprawling indefinite stain, caused no doubt by some leak long since stopped in the roof overhead, but it possessed in Jane's eyes the weird peculiarity of assuming various pictorial shapes which matched the girl's own passing experiences. Once she remembered seeing in it a train of gypsy wagons, with a peculiarly alluring and picturesque gypsy plodding on before—this in the days when she longed to run away, yet did not quite dare for fear of being caught and brought back ignominiously to taste the sharp sting of the ferrule, which lay darkly in wait for evil doers in the upper left-hand drawer of Lady Agatha's private desk.

Of late years the stain had assumed the appearance of a mountain valley, with a lofty castle perched high amid inaccessible cliffs. There was a long series of romances connected with this imaginary abode, in every one of which Jane herself, in a robe of white samite, bound about the waist with a girdle of red gold, figured as heroine. Sometimes a hostile army, their spears and pennants showing dimly through the trees, would defile stealthily through the dark passes, to intrench themselves before the castle moat, where Jane would parley with them, intrepid and unblenching in a glistening coat of chain armor fitting her lithe figure like a serpent's skin. Again, a solitary knight with closed visor overshadowed by ebon plumes could be seen pulling in his foaming charger below the embattled terraces awaiting a glimpse of the white figure above.

On this particular morning beetling cliffs, castle and all had vanished and Jane, rubbing the dreams from her eyes, beheld a wide expanse of tumbling ocean, with a sky piled high with flying clouds, and in the foreground, ploughing its way through the foam, a stately ship. Jane stared unwinkingly at the vision for a long minute, then her eyes descended in startled haste to the floor, where rested the locked and strapped box, with O. A. B. in white letters on its end. Jane sat up in the bed with a queer choking in her slender throat. If Oliver Aubrey-Blythe were alive, his one daughter would not be driven forth friendless into the wide world to make her difficult way.

Twenty minutes later, refreshed by her bath and dressed in the gown she had chosen for her travels, Jane was quite her cheerful self again. She was also unromantically hungry, and after a brief period of indecision descended boldly to the breakfast room, where she was tolerably certain of finding none of the female members of the household.

Mr. Robert Aubrey-Blythe was apparently just about finishing his repast and his newspaper. He looked up as his niece entered the room. "Good morning, Jane," he said fussily. "You are late."

"Yes, Uncle Robert," very meekly, "I overslept this morning."

"I—er—in short, Jane, I saw Towle again yesterday, at the Club," pursued Mr. Aubrey-Blythe, thoughtfully gazing at the girl through his double eyeglasses. "The man is—er—quite daft about you, Jane. I own I was astonished. Ha-ha! very amusing, I'm sure."

"I'll never speak to Mr. Towle again—*never*!" cried Jane, her cheeks flaming. "The idea of his daring——"

"Tut-tut, girl; don't be a fool!" advised Mr. Aubrey-Blythe testily. "What Towle said was—er—quite correct, quite as it should be, in case—you—er—. By the by, Jane, why can't you hit it off better with Lady Agatha and Gwendolyn? I'm infernally bored with having to hear about your interminable squabbles; I am, indeed. And it's beastly bad taste in you, Jane, to be always getting up scenes. You ought to know that."

"There'll be no further scenes between Gwendolen and myself," said Jane, very calm and dignified. "I can promise you that, sir."

"Well now, upon my word, that sounds something like," said Mr. Aubrey-Blythe, pushing back his chair. "I trust you'll keep that in mind hereafter. We—er—shall endeavor to do our duty by you, Jane; and you, on your part——"

The girl's sudden and unexpected response to this well-meant attempt at reconciliation shocked and astonished her worthy relative beyond measure. She arose from her chair and put her two young arms about his neck with something very like a sob. "I do thank you, Uncle Robert, for all you've done for me," she said. "I've not meant to be disagreeable or ungrateful since I've lived in your house; indeed I've not. But I—couldn't help it, and I'm sorry for—everything!"

"Come—come—er—I say!" spluttered Mr. Aubrey-Blythe. "You mustn't, you know, or I shall have to call Lady Agatha. I dare say you'll go on quite as you should after this."

"Good-by, uncle," said Jane, smiling and winking fast to keep the tears from falling off her thick lashes. "I'm glad I said it. You'll not forget."

Then she sat down with a very good appetite to the fresh coffee and eggs and bacon which were set before her. One must eat to live, however young and beautiful one may be, and whatever the base and undeserved cruelty of one's relations. She had not finished when Percy and Cecil clattered into the breakfast room, with every evidence of having carried on a spirited skirmish on the way downstairs.

"Hello, Jane, you here?" growled Cecil, drawing a long face. "We're to have no lessons to-day, mind!"

"Who said so?" inquired Miss Blythe tranquilly.

"Mamma said so. She said you were going to be sent away directly, and we're to go away to school. Hooray!"

"I don't want to go to school," whined Percy dismally. "I want Jane."

"Shut up, baby; you don't know what you're talkin' about. I don't want Jane, an' I'm glad the mater's goin' to ship her; so there! Here, you, Calkins, fetch us some hot muffins; these ain't fit to eat. And, I say, hustle some marmalade while you're about it!"

Miss Blythe arose from her place. "If you can't ask civilly for your food, Cecil, you don't deserve to have anything fetched," she said rebukingly.

"Cecil's a cad, anyhow," muttered Percy, staring truculently at his brother from under his light lashes.

"Aw! an' you're a bally baby!" retorted Master Cecil, stuffing half a muffin into his cheek. "My, won't you catch it in school, though!"

"See here, boys," said Jane seriously, "very likely I'll not see you again, for I am going away——"

"You're to be *sent*, you mean," interrupted Cecil impudently.

"Be quiet, sir, and pay attention to what I have to say; it's the last time I shall take the trouble. You, Percy, have the instincts of a gentleman. If you'll go on telling the truth every trip, no matter what bully threatens you, and if you'll stand for what's decent and right you'll have nothing to fear, in school or anywhere else. As for you, Cecil, you've a lot to learn, and I heartily hope the big boys will thrash your meanness and cowardliness out of you before you're entirely spoiled, and I dare say they will. Good-by."

She stooped to kiss Percy warmly, and that small boy blubbered outright as he rubbed his smeary little face against the girl's smooth cheek. To Cecil she offered her hand, but withdrew it with a smile, as the grateful recipient of her counsels thrust his tongue into his cheek with a frightful grimace. "Good-by, boys," she repeated. "You'll find what I've told you is true before you've done."

It was a long, lonely day, passed in a dreary attempt to hasten the lagging hours with one of Susan's "shilling shockers," which that worthy damsel had pressed upon her adored young lady's attention as being "perfec'ly el'gant an' that thrillin' it ud raise yer 'air to read it." Jane found "The Duke's Revenge, or the Secret of the Hidden Staircase" insufficient to keep her wandering attention from the water stain on the ceiling, which by this time had assumed the appearance of a coach and pair careering at full gallop on the verge of a precipice. She passed the morning in momently dreading a summons from Lady Agatha, but none came, and after luncheon (which Jane decided to omit) peeping from her lofty window she caught a glimpse of that stately matron and her daughter magnificently attired sailing forth to their carriage. Later in the day she beheld the Hon. Wipplinger Towle, immaculately groomed and wearing a gardenia in his buttonhole, advancing up the street.

Ten minutes later Susan tapped at the door, the proud bearer of a slim white card on a diminutive salver. "I told Jeems as 'ow I thought I'd find you 'ere, miss," she said.

"You may say that I'm not at home, if you please, Susan," said Jane.

But Susan stood still in her tracks. "'Is 'air ain't much to brag of, I know, miss," she ventured at length; "an' 'e can't be called 'an'some in other pertic'lers, but I ain't sure as I wouldn't tak' up wi' 'im, seein' there ain't no lord nor dook 'andy. 'E's a gent'man, that 'e is; 'an you'd be a-ridin' in a kerridge o' yer own wi' nobody to worrit you, an' *me* lidy's maid a-waitin' on you constant, instead of occasional like, as I'm forced now along wi' my reg'lar dooties."

Jane laughed outright. "You're a good soul, Susan," she said; "but your advice isn't exactly to my taste. Go down at once and do as I've told you. Later I've something to say to you; and I shall want your help, too."

By this Susan's eyes had lighted upon Jane's modest box, which stood locked and strapped for its long journey at the foot of Jane's little bed. "Oh, Miss Jane Evelyn," she blubbered, "you ain't a-goin' away!"

"I must," said Jane. "I can't stay here any longer. I'll tell you about it when you come up again. You must go down directly now and tell James to excuse me to Mr. Towle."

But James was engaged in parleying with another visitor when Susan arrived at the level of the reception room, and after an instant's reflection she smoothed down her immaculate apron, touched up the frills of her cap, and boldly presented herself before the Hon. Wipplinger Towle, who was waiting with his wonted middle-aged patience.

"Miss Jane Evelyn's be'n took bad wi' a wi'lent 'eadache, sir, an' will you kindly excuse 'er, sir." And Susan bobbed her very best courtesy.

Mr. Towle stood up and fixed his glass in his eye. "Hum—ah! I am very sorry to hear it. You will—er—tell Miss Aubrey-Blythe so, with my compliments, my good girl."

"Yes, sir; I will, sir; an' thank you kindly, sir," said Susan, slipping something into her apron pocket, with a broad grin.

Mr. Towle appeared to be gazing rebukingly at the frills on Susan's cap; but that astute damsel knew better than to withdraw too hastily. Presently he spoke again. "You are—ah—Susan; are you not?"

"Yes, sir; thank you, sir. I ain't nobody else but Susan, sir," beamed the girl encouragingly. "An' I'm that fond of Miss Jane Evelyn, if you'll believe it, sir, 'as I'd lay down willin' i' the mud an' let her walk over me, that I would, sir!"

"Hum—ah!" murmured the Hon. Mr. Towle, "that is very good of you, I'm sure, Susan; most praiseworthy, in short. Do you—er—attend Miss Blythe when she—er—travels? She is going out of town, I believe."

"I don't know no mor'n nothink what Miss Jane Evelyn's a-goin' to do, sir. I'd give me heyes to go wi' 'er; that I would; but I'll not be let, sir."

"Then you don't know where she is going?"

"No, sir; not yet, sir; but she'll tell me, sure, afore ever she goes. I 'ate to say it as I shouldn't, but Miss Jane Evelyn 'arsn't many friends in this 'ere 'ouse but me an' cook an' may'ap Master Percy, 'im bein' the youngest of hall. I 'ear below stairs as 'ow she's to be sent off somewheres directly, sir, an' the young lads'll go to school hafter she's gone wot teached 'em faithful since the las' gov'ness went away."

"Hum—ah," mused Mr. Towle, scowling fiercely. "I say," he added abruptly, "this doesn't seem a very civil thing for me to do; but it's important I should know where Miss—er—your young mistress goes. I might be able to be of service to her, you know."

"Yes, sir; I gets your meanin' quite, sir," pursued the ecstatic Susan, feeling herself to be nothing less than confidential lady in a real, live novel of absorbing interest. "I'll let you know, sir, as soon as ever I finds out, an' find out I will, sir; you may depend upon it, sir."

"Thank you, Susan, my good girl; do so by all means," said Mr. Towle; then a second something clinked against the first in an adjacent apron pocket.

After which Susan sped up the stairs as fast as her feet could carry her, to find Miss Jane Evelyn calmly putting on her hat and veil before her little mirror.

"I wish you would call a cab for me, directly, Susan," said the young lady; "and could you help me carry this box down to the area door, do you think?"

"Oh, Miss Jane Evelyn, where *are* you goin'?" implored Susan, wild-eyed with haste and sudden alarm. "Don't do nothink rash, I himplore you, miss!"

"Don't be a goose, Susan; but do as you're bid. I have arranged to travel in America with a—lady. And you must help me get away out of the house without a scene; there's a good girl."

Susan sighed deeply. She was as wax in Miss Jane Evelyn's hands, and she knew it. "Does the missus know where you're a-goin', miss?" she ventured to inquire.

"No, Susan," Jane told her firmly. "I have decided to look out for myself from now on; I am plenty old enough." Miss Blythe looked very tall and dignified as she said this, and Susan went meekly away to call the cab, fingering Mr. Towle's money as she did so with an air of guilty reserve.

It was quite dusk when Jane's modest luggage was finally strapped atop the cab, and Jane herself was seated within. Poor Susan stood blubbering at the curb. "I wisht to 'eavin's you'd think better of it, Miss Jane Evelyn," she whimpered. "I 'ate to see you a-goin' hoff like this wi' nobody to say good-by but me, an' a nice gent'man likely a-breakin' 'is 'eart to bits when 'e finds you're gone."

"Pooh!" said Jane, rather faintly; "he'll not care. Nobody will care but you, my good Susan. Good-by, *dear, dear* Susan! And thank you again for everything you've always been doing for me!"

"Oh, Miss Jane Evelyn, if you do be set on goin'—as I see you be, I 'ope as 'ow you'll 'ave a most 'eavinly time, an' come back merried to a rich gent'man—for they do say as 'ow all the gents in Hamerica is a-rollin' in gold an' di'mon's; an' 'eavin knows you deserve the best of heverythink, Miss Jane Evelyn; that you do! God bless you, miss, an' thank you kindly! Good-by!"

Then the cabby slammed the door and Jane found herself rolling away to Belgravia Crescent, where Mrs. Markle, clad in a voluminous traveling cloak and heavily veiled, was waiting to join her. Mrs. Markle pressed the girl's hand in her fat, moist palm. "I was beginning to fear you would not, after all, come wiz me, dear child," she said sweetly. "I should have wept wiz ze disappointment."

Once on board ship Mrs. Markle's manner changed perceptibly. "You will not bozzer me while at sea," she said to Jane, rather sharply, "*not—at—all—* you comprend? I am seeck—ah! I suffer wiz ze *mal de mer*, an' I not talk—nevaire. You sleep in anozzer cabin—ze stewardess she will show you. But stay, your jacket iss too—what you call it—too theen—not war-rm for the sea. It iss so cold—ugh! see! I make you warm wiz zis." And Mrs. Markle drew from her steamer trunk a luxurious fur-lined cloak which she threw upon Jane's slender shoulders.

"Do you mean that you want me to wear this cloak?" asked Jane, astonished beyond measure. "Oh, thank you! You are very kind; but I think my own jacket will be quite comfortable. I could not wear a borrowed garment."

The woman was smiling broadly, but the smile slowly faded as she stared at Jane's flushed face.

"Eh—but w'y not?" she demanded. "You evaire cross ze ocean before zis?"

"No," confessed Jane; "but——"

"Zen you do as I say. You would fr-r-eeze in zis sing," and she fingered Jane's modest wrap contemptuously. "Come," she murmured persuasively; "you will please me—yes? I ha-a-te to have anyone wiz me feel ze discomfort. Ah, now, see!"

Jane blushed resentfully, then sighed, as the luxurious folds fell about her little figure.

"Why, it just fits me!" she exclaimed in an astonished voice.

"*Certainment!*" smiled the woman, passing her fat, jeweled fingers complacently over the girl's shoulders. "I am very good judge of ze figure. I was sure it would fit."

"What, did you buy it for me?" cried Jane, quite overcome by such kindness.

"Why sure I did!" purred the woman. "An' ze leetle cap, too—see?" And she settled a coquetish yachting cap into place on Jane's head. "Ze hats wiz fezzers, zey blow into bits an' fly away at sea. You leave zis leetle coat an' hat wiz me till we come in port, zen I gif zem to you alright. But mind, you mus' not spik to anybody on ze ship—*not—one—word—of—me*! You un'erstan'—eh?"

Jane stared at the woman's scowling face with something like fear. But as she looked the frown on Mrs. Markle's large face melted into quick laughter. "You're alright—alright, a real nize young lady," she murmured, "you will not spik to men or to any womans—no, nevaire. Go now, an' make ze voyage. I see you once every day after ze *dejeuner*."

Jane stepped out rather uncertainly into the brilliantly lighted corridor beyond the stateroom door, then paused with a startled face. Something strange and powerful had begun to throb in the unknown depths beneath her feet, slowly at first, then steadying to a monotonous beat—beat. The screw of the great ship, which was to bear her to new and strange experiences beyond the sea, was in motion.

Several hours later Lady Agatha returning from a dinner party, very much out of temper because her hostess had stupidly given the rich American wife of an up-country baronet precedence over her, found a note skewered to her cushion with a big black-headed hat pin (Susan's device, borrowed from a shilling shocker).

> "Aunt Agatha:" (she read) "I am going to America, and as I do not intend to return, you will have no further reason to regret my 'unfortunate influence' over your children.
>
> "Please say good-by to Percy for me. He is a *real Aubrey-Blythe*, and I am sorry that I shall never see him again. But I shall not pretend that I am sorry to be leaving your house. You will be glad to be rid of me, I know; and I am equally glad of this opportunity of going away. So we are quits.
>
> "You seemed to feel that I do not appreciate what you have done for me in the past. I think I have and do appreciate *everything*; I have thought of little else of late. And this has led quite directly to my present determination. Good-by, good-by!
>
> "JANE EVELYN AUBREY-BLYTHE."

On the day following, the Hon. Wipplinger Towle was likewise the recipient of a communication, the contents of which he finally deciphered with difficulty. It was written on pink paper, strongly scented with cheap perfumery, and was fetched to his lodgings, so his man informed him, "by a very respectable appearin' pusson in blue an' scarlet livery."

"i sed as ow i wud leve yu no, sir, wen mis Jane Evelyn went away,"—he read—"shes gon to America, that is awl i no, sir, she went suddint, or i wud ave towld yu. if i ad munny i wud follo. if the shu fitz, put it awn. Susan Haythorne."

CHAPTER VI

The six days of the voyage passed uneventfully enough. Jane Blythe, obeying Mrs. Markle's instructions, spoke to no one, and although one or two women, muffled to their eyes in wraps, stared at her in sleepy curiosity from their steamer chairs, and an elderly man restored her head covering, which on one occasion escaped its moorings and blew across the deck, no one attempted to enter into conversation with her. Jane accepted this circumstance as she accepted everything else in her new and strange surroundings. She ate regularly, which could be said of very few of the other passengers, and slept soundly at night after long, delightful days spent on deck in the keen mid-ocean air, and with it all her thin face rounded into a lovely radiance of girlish bloom, which caused the retiring Mrs. Markle to exclaim in fretful amazement.

That lady's large, flaccid countenance had assumed a peculiar, olive-green tint which the glaring electric lights in her cabin accentuated to an unpleasant ghastliness. She was very short in her communications with Jane in the brief interviews which took place each day after luncheon.

"You spik to anyone since I see you—*n'est-ce-pas?*" she would demand, staring eagerly at Jane from the midst of her pillows. "*Non? Tres bien!* say nossing to womans asking questions; to mens, nossing. I ha-a-te zem all."

"But no one has spoken to me, except to say 'good morning' at the table," Jane made haste to assure her.

"Alright—*tres bien*," muttered Mrs. Markle. "Go now—*vite*! and to-morrow—no, next day, we come in port. Zen I tell you one leetle sing you do for me."

"I have done nothing for you yet," replied Jane, in genuine distress. "Would you not like me to read aloud to you for a while, or bathe your head with cologne? I should be so glad to do something to make you comfortable."

But Mrs. Markle waved her aside with a fretful motion of her dingy, jeweled hands. "Go; make ze voyage as you like. I want nossing—nossing till we come in port. Zen I say what you mus' do. A mos' leetle sing, I tell you."

On the last day when the women passengers were beginning to look less like rows of Egyptian mummies put out for an airing, and a buzz of cheerful conversation pervaded the decks and cabins, Jane was astonished to find Mrs. Markle sitting in her stateroom, fully dressed and elaborately frizzled and coiffured, as on the day she had first seen her.

"Oh, are you better? I am so glad!" exclaimed Jane. "Won't you come up on deck for a while, and see all the people?"

"*Non!*" snorted Mrs. Markle. "I will not. I am not able to walk yet. I am—what you call it—we-e-k from ze illness. Now leesten to *moi*, I gif you your hat an' coat. Put zem on, an' leave ze fur wiz me. Zen stay in cabin till ze customs officer comes aboard. You have no articles dutiable—*non*?"

Jane stared at her in mute amazement. "I don't—know," she stammered.

"Have you di'mon's, watches, fezzers—laces—eh?" sneered Mrs. Markle, "kid gloves, silks, bronzes—in your so leetle box?—*non*? Say so, zen; when zey ask you. Zes so gra-a-nd United Sta-a-tes mek you pay—*comprenez?*—for all such sings. An' see, before we land at ze dock, you come back to me here. I s'all ask you to help wiz ze luggage."

But Jane was not asked to carry anything, when at last, the big ship securely fast at her dock, the two prepared to go ashore.

"See, now, Jane," said Mrs. Markle, "zere is one leetle sing I wis' not to lose—a so small package. Do you mek it safe inside your jacket, so it be not lost for me. I haf no place to keep it. Do not take it out. Say nossing to nobody. I gif you money ven you gif it safe to *moi*. Zen in ze customs, you will go by your box in ze place marked 'B'; I mus' stay in 'M.' After all is passed we go on. You haf nossing dutiable— I haf nossing; we are quick through. Zen we go to see ze so gr-r-and sights in America—*oui*!"

Jane permitted the woman to fasten a flat package, securely wrapped in soft paper, in the loose folds of her blouse. Then the two made their way to the deck, and from thence across the gang plank into the great, noisy place, where the luggage of the passengers was being rapidly sorted into vast piles.

As Mrs. Markle had predicted, they seemed likely to be quickly passed through the customhouse. Jane's modest luggage was thrown down almost at her feet, and, following Mrs. Markle's careful directions, she at once drew the attention of a waiting official to it.

The man gruffly demanded her keys; unlocked the trunk; rumpled its scant contents with a perfunctory hand; replaced it; scribbled a cabalistic design upon its lid with a piece of chalk. Then, as if moved by an after thought, he turned to the girl who stood looking on.

"Have you anything dutiable about your person?" he asked sharply; "any jewelry—laces—or such like?"

"I have my locket with my father's picture," confessed Jane, trembling, "and mother's wedding ring; oh, sir, please don't take them away from me. They'd be no good to anyone but me."

The man was gazing at her keenly. Something in his stern eyes reminded Jane of the mysterious flat package Mrs. Markle had given into her charge.

"And I have a—a small parcel, too," she faltered; "I don't know what is in it."

"Give it to me; I'll soon tell you," said the man grimly.

"It doesn't belong to me, sir," added Jane, trembling still more as the inspector's practiced fingers quickly undid the wrappings.

Then she stared in astonishment as the man shook out yards and yards of costly, filmy lace.

"You didn't know what was in it—eh?"

"No, sir," said Jane.

"Where did you get it, miss?"

"The lady I am traveling with asked me to carry it for her," faltered Jane. "Oh, but I mustn't lose it. You must give it to me directly. I am sure it looks very valuable."

"You're right it does," said the man grimly. "I guess you'll have to come with me, young woman, and we'll see what else you're carrying for the lady."

"Oh, I've nothing else!" protested Jane, "and Mrs. Markle is waiting for me; I see her now."

"Where?" demanded the official, keenly alert. "Point her out to me!"

"The large lady yonder with the long cloak—. Oh, she is looking at me now! I am afraid she will be displeased about the lace. But of course, I had to tell you when you asked me."

"Of course!" echoed the man, with a sneer, "the ladies are always careful to tell me everything of the sort. Now, you'll go with this woman; she'll look into your case. And I'll just step across and speak to Mrs. Markle."

The next hour in Jane Blythe's history is best passed over in pitying silence. At the end of it a pallid, tremulous girl was confronting a stern-faced official to whom she related in detail the circumstances of her short acquaintance with Mrs. Markle.

"She asked you to leave your hat and jacket in her cabin, did she?" he interrupted sharply, at one point in the narrative.

"She said it was too thin for the sea," Jane told him. "She was very kind and loaned me a warm cloak lined with fur."

"Did you notice anything peculiar about your own jacket when you put it on to leave the ship?"

"No, sir," said Jane; "I was too much taken up with having reached America to notice that it was thicker and lumpy in spots."

"It was very neatly done," put in the female inspector, whose name was Forbes. "The woman had ample time during the voyage to quilt thousands of dollars' worth of laces between the lining and the outside. It is evidently an old game successfully played before this."

Then she stepped to one side to make room for a second inspector who entered from the rear accompanied by Mrs. Markle herself, unbending and majestic.

"I s'all complain of zis outra—a—ge! You s'all be arrest, *bêtes*, animals—all!" announced Mrs. Markle in a shrill, high-pitched voice. "Zere was nossing dutiable in my luggage—I was alright *aussi—n'est-ce pas?*"

The woman inspector shrugged her shoulders. "I found nothing," she agreed. "But—" She glanced expressively at Jane who had fixed her clear hazel eyes reproachfully upon Mrs. Markle.

"Is this the person in whose employ you crossed from England?" demanded the presiding official of Jane.

"Yes, sir, this is Mrs. Markle," replied Jane politely.

"*Lies!—all lies!*" snapped the stout woman. "Nevaire before have I seen zis young woman. My name is Madame Melbrun. I dema-a-nd my release *immediatement*. Zis adventuress is a stra-a-nger to *moi*; I have nossing to do wiz her."

Jane's eyes opened wide with shocked surprise. "Oh!" she cried. "How can you say that?"

Mrs. Markle had folded her fat hands across her capacious form with an air of haughty innocence. She did not once look at Jane. "I have no articles dutiable," she repeated. "I am first-class passenger—name Madame Melbrun—you find it so on ze passenger list. I dem-a-and my r-r-rights!"

"Let her go," ordered the presiding official, shrugging his shoulders, "she's got us; but then we've got her, too."

Mrs. Markle swept out without so much as a glance in Jane's direction; nevertheless that young person shivered a little as if conscious of the woman's murderous thoughts.

The inspector was writing something in a ledger with a pen which scratched sharply. He raised his eyes as the pen ceased its mordant protest. "You may go," he said to Jane.

"Where may I go?" asked the girl piteously.

"Anywhere you like," returned the inspector briskly. "You are free. Better keep out of Madame Melbrun's way, though. You owe her something like five thousand dollars, and she'd like to collect. Better be more careful in your choice of mistresses next time you hire out, young woman."

The woman inspector looked pityingly at Jane. "You come with me," she said. "I'll help you put your jacket together again."

Bertha Forbes was as good as her word, and better. When she found Jane had no friends in America and little money, she took her to her own boarding house in a narrow, dirty street near the North River pier, and later introduced her to a reliable employment agency.

Jane was far too young and inexperienced in the ways of the great and wicked city of New York to be suitably grateful for these kind offices; but she thanked Miss Forbes warmly, even while she declined to follow her later counsels.

"You'd better go back to your aunt," Miss Forbes had said grimly. "It isn't pleasant to be snubbed by rich relatives, I'll admit, but it's far better than—some other things I could tell you of; and I'll see to the transportation."

Jane set her small white teeth. "I'll not go back to Aunt Agatha," she murmured passionately. "I am strong—far stronger than I look. I can work."

"Very good," said Bertha Forbes, who was merely a lonely, good-hearted woman, when she was off duty. "I'll help you get a place."

But the stars in their courses seemed to fight against Jane. There were numbers of persons indeed who were looking for a "refined young woman, English preferred," to act as nursery governess; but, unluckily, the refined and undeniably attractive Miss Blythe had no references beyond a manly-looking scrawl of Bertha Forbes's composition, in which Jane was described as being a young English woman known to the writer as a well-educated person of good, moral character.

"I am afraid," said Jane, with an ingenuous blush, "that it hurts your conscience to say all that about me, considering the circumstances of our first acquaintance."

"No," said Miss Forbes, "my conscience is not of the abnormally sensitive variety, in the first place; in the second, I am morally certain that you are exactly what you say you are. But the truth is, my good girl, that my convictions, while entirely satisfactory to myself, will not hold water if it comes to investigating them, and the people who are willing to pay well for having their children kept out of their way are quite apt to investigate. It gives them an easy conscience, you see."

Added to this unconvincing dimness of her immediate background was Jane's ingrained habit of telling the truth upon occasions when an elusive reticence would have been far more prudent.

One impulsive lady, it is true, was about to engage Jane out of hand, being irresistibly attracted by her smile and manner. But before concluding the matter she chanced to ask Miss Blythe why she had come to America.

"I came to America," said Jane, endeavoring to be discreet "because I was—very unhappy in England."

"Indeed!" exclaimed Mrs. Newport, scenting a mystery, "and why were you unhappy in England?"

Jane was silent for a space. "I don't see why I should tell you," she said at last, with a proud lifting of her little head; "my troubles concerned no one but myself."

Mrs. Newport raised her eyebrows. "I must *insist* upon knowing everything about your past," she said conclusively, "else I cannot engage you."

Jane arose with the air of a duchess in disguise. "Good morning, Mrs. Newport," she said.

Bertha Forbes shook her head when she heard of this circumstance. "I'm sorry you didn't see fit to tell the woman something about yourself," she said. "There is really nothing to be ashamed of in your story, except the smuggling part—that I'd advise you to keep to yourself."

"No," said Jane stonily. "I have nothing to be ashamed of; but the fact that I wish to work for my living does not give that woman, or any other, the right to ask impertinent questions about my private affairs."

"Why, yes," disagreed Miss Forbes dryly; "it does. Mrs. Newport was about to engage you to play the young mother to her three darlings, while she golfed and motored and otherwise disported her fashionable self; the very least she could do was to assure herself of your fitness for the position. And this involved a knowledge of your Alpha as well as your Omega; you see that; don't you?"

Being very far from stupid, Jane saw, and when, on the following day, Mrs. Narragansett's housekeeper interviewed Miss Blythe, that young person was prepared to be frank and open to the point of telling all her pitiful little story.

"My name," she began, in response to Mrs. Pott's initial question, "is Jane Evelyn Aubrey-Blythe."

Mrs. Potts bestowed a supercilious glance upon the young person. "And what was your last position as nursery governess?" she further demanded.

"I taught my cousins, Percy and Cecil Aubrey-Blythe, in London and at Blythe Court."

"Indeed! And why did you leave that situation, *if* you please?"

Jane drew a quick breath. "Must I answer that question?" she entreated, blushing hotly, a circumstance which the experienced Mrs. Potts noted with growing disfavor.

"You certainly must," that lady assured her with business-like coldness.

"I—I thought my aunt was unkind to me," faltered Jane, with every appearance of guilt. "I was very much vexed with her and—and with my Cousin Gwendolen, and so——"

"Your aunt's name, if you please? And you may also state the occasion of her being unkind to you."

"My aunt's name is Lady Agatha Aubrey-Blythe," said Jane, endeavoring to pull herself together with very little success. "She was unkind to me because—because— She accused me of— No; I—I cannot tell you."

"It is quite unnecessary, Miss—Aubrey-Blythe," Mrs. Potts assured her, with an unpleasant smile. "You are not, I am sure, a suitable person for the situation. Good morning."

Jane wept a little when she confided this last failure to Bertha Forbes's sympathizing ear. "I couldn't tell that woman what Aunt Agatha said to me about Mr. Towle; now, could I?"

"She wouldn't have believed it, if you had," said Miss Forbes gruffly. "Better try another tack," she added, still more gruffly. "Better yet, go back to your uncle. He can't be a bad sort, from what you tell me."

"Uncle Robert? Oh, no! he is—he has never been unkind to me. I—I quite love Uncle Robert; that is to say, I should love to love him, if he would let me."

"Then you'll go back to England like a sensible girl; tell your uncle you've made a fool of yourself, but you'll try not to do it again. Think it over till tomorrow morning, and remember I'll take care of the transportation."

Jane reflected upon this eminently sane proposition over night; then she faced her new-found friend and advisor with a pale but determined face.

"Thank you for offering to pay my passage back to England," she said, "but I really can't accept it. I couldn't face Aunt Agatha and Gwendolen and—and the others. I'd rather scrub floors than to do that! Perhaps I'll have to scrub in the end, for my money is almost gone."

Bertha Forbes stared at the girl speculatively. "If you will tell them at the employment agency that you're willing to do house work, you'll soon find a place," she said; "there are plenty of people who will hire you to work in their houses, and ask few questions about your past. But it's no fun to scrub floors, my young friend, unless the floors happen to be your own. I never tried *that* myself; but I've seen deluded young women who seemed to think it a vastly agreeable pastime, if there was only a young man in the case."

And this is how it came about that Miss Jane Evelyn Aubrey-Blythe—just two weeks from the time she informed the invisible forces of the universe that things would have to change—found herself humbly seeking entrance at the side door of a modest, detached villa, situated in a modest, detached suburb of New York. "Things" had changed, indeed!

CHAPTER VII

There was, apparently, no one at home in the modest detached villa; for, although Jane could hear the trill of the electric bell within, the door remained fast shut. After a discreet interval she ventured to sit down for a minute's rest on a little green bench set beneath the budding vines. Then she drew a deep breath. It was very quiet, and the air blowing over wide expanses of vacant lots was sweet and warm. Dandelions were in bloom amid the green April grass, and an American robin sang loudly in a tall elm near the front gate. Jane looked about her with a homesick flutter of her sore heart. The raw suburb, with its muddy road, its hastily constructed sidewalks, its ornate houses with their protruding balconies, bay-windows and hideous roof lines, broken by extraneous ornamental railings and dormer windows of no known style of architecture, offended eyes accustomed to the garden trimness and ordered beauty of England.

Bertha Forbes's parting advice recurred to her mind with an added touch of poignancy: "It may not be pleasant to be snubbed by one's rich relations; but it's better than some other things I know of."

Jane wondered—for a fleeting minute—if she had made a fool of herself. If, after all, she would not better have endured accustomed woes than to fly to ills she knew not of.

But such tardy reflections were speedily ended by the sound of voices and footsteps from the rear. Jane rose hastily to her feet just in time to behold a tall, broad-shouldered young man appear around the corner of the veranda at an ambling trot, while a small boy of two or three plied a switch about his heels and jerked the scarlet lines attached to his person.

"Det-tup!" shouted the boy vociferously. "Det-tup, I say!"

But the young man had already caught sight of Jane. "Hold on, Buster," he said, turning to the child, "till I speak to the lady. Did you ring?" he added, addressing Jane, with a polite bow.

"Yes," she told him; "but no one answered. I wish to see Mrs. Belknap—on business," she added hastily.

"Ah, yes," he returned, apparently absorbed in his contemplation of Jane's undeniable beauty. "Mrs. Belknap is not at home; but—oh, don't go—er—she'll be at home soon. In fact, she told me she was expecting some one, and asked me to——"

"I think she expected me," said Jane coldly. "I am the new maid—that is, if I suit."

The young man stared incredulously. "I—I beg your pardon," he stammered, a wave of color passing over his boyish face. "I don't know what you'll think of me; but I—er—fancied you were a friend of Mrs. Belknap's. She was expected this afternoon, and I———"

"No; I am the maid," said Jane haughtily. "If Mrs. Belknap is coming home directly, I will wait here till she comes."

She sat down again on the green bench and fixed her hazel eyes on the remote distance.

The small boy threw down his whip and climbed up the steps. "I want a piece of bwead an' butter," he said confidentially, "an' I want a dwink of water, an' I want———"

"Buster!" called the young man warningly. "Come here!"

But the infant paid no heed. "I want a piece of bwead an' butter," he repeated in a louder voice, "an' I want a dwink of water, an' I want———"

"Were you speaking to me?" inquired Jane, withdrawing her eyes from the safe horizon and looking down at the child.

"Yeth," he assented, "I want a piece of bwead an' butter, an' I want a dwink of water, an' I———"

"Come with me, Buster! I'll get them for you," volunteered the young man. He was deliberately divesting himself of the scarlet harness. "Won't you come in?" he went on, turning to Jane. "I see it's beginning to rain."

Reluctantly she passed in at the door he held wide for her. "Please sit down," he urged. "I'm sure Mrs. Belknap will be at home very soon. She's only gone out for an hour or so."

"I want a d-w-i-nk!" vociferated the small boy.

"Yes, I gathered as much from your remarks; come on, old fellow."

Jane sat down, and the young man and the child disappeared into the unknown regions beyond. Jane could hear the boy's shrill voice, and the deeper replies of the man. Her cheeks were very red, and she sat stiffly erect. She felt unreasonably vexed with herself, with the child, but most of all with the young man. He was unlike any masculine person of her acquaintance, she reflected; still he had spoken to her very civilly, though not in the tone a gentleman should use to an inferior. But was he, after all, a gentleman? These class distinctions were said to be very puzzling in America, Jane remembered. She resolved not to speak to this particular young American again. It would not, she concluded sagely, be the correct thing to do.

A distant crash of breaking crockery, an infantile shriek, an exclamation of deep dismay preceded a hasty opening of the closed door. The ingenuous countenance of the man was thrust hastily within. "Oh, I beg your pardon! but could you come out and—er—help me a minute? Buster has tipped the milk all over himself, and I—oh, please do—that's a good girl—. I don't know what in thunder—. Hold hard, old fellow, I'm coming!"

The last by way of reply to the frenzied shrieks of rage and despair which issued from the rear.

Jane's austere expression relaxed perceptibly as she surveyed the agitated and imploring countenance of the young American.

"Oh, thanks; you're awfully good!" he was saying, as Jane arose, preparatory to accompanying him to the scene of the disaster. "I just set the bowl of milk on the table, you know—he wanted milk by the time we had reached the commissariat—and while I was hustling for the bread, he reached up to investigate and—you see what followed."

The infant was seated in a pool of milk on the floor; milk dripped slowly from his flaxen curls, the tip of his chubby nose, and his pink cheeks. His round fists were applied to his milky eyes, while his rosy mouth emitted scream after scream of anguish.

"Is he hurt?" inquired Jane, in a business-like tone.

"He must have caught a whack of the bowl as it fell, I suppose," admitted the man. "What shall we do?"

Jane had already helped herself to an apron which hung conveniently near; she turned up her cuffs. "A towel and a basin, please," she suggested. Then she stooped over the howling infant and lifted him gently to his feet.

"Do 'way!" he shrieked, thrashing out vigorously with fists and feet; "I want my muzzer!"

Jane skillfully evaded the attacks, while she plied the towel with a calm mastery of the situation, which roused the wonder and warm admiration of the man.

"Just quit that kicking, won't you, Buster?" he suggested, in a conciliatory tone. "I declare, I believe I've found a—stick of candy—no—but it's a nickel to buy one with."

The magic word so mendaciously inserted acted with its accustomed power. Jane, busy with her beneficent offices in which the towel and basin played a conspicuous part, scarcely noticed the fact that the young American, whom she had so recently decided to ignore, was kneeling close at her side apparently intent upon a well-meant attempt at assistance.

"Why, Jack Everett—what in the world!" exclaimed an unfamiliar voice from the doorway.

All three participants in the late tragedy raised their eyes to the pretty and—to Jane's notion—somewhat too smartly dressed young woman, who was surveying the scene in an attitude of extreme surprise.

The man rose rather shamefacedly to his feet; the small boy, breaking away from Jane, dashed forward with a loud, ecstatic whoop to precipitate himself and his milky pinafore upon the lady; while Jane hastily turned down her cuffs, a deep flush of vexation mounting to her forehead.

"I 'pilled all 'e milk, muzzer!" shouted the infant. "Zen I bumped my head, an' I *cwied* an' I *cwied*!"

"Where is Mary?" demanded the newcomer.

"Mary has just 'shtipped out for a minut'," explained the young man mildly. "She announced her intention of doing so shortly after you left the house. Buster and I have been keeping house as well as we knew how; and then—this—er—young lady——"

"I am the maid from the Streeter agency," said Jane distinctly. She felt sure now that the man was not a gentleman; she also decided that she disliked him exceedingly.

"Oh!" murmured the lady, turning a keenly penetrating and speculative gaze upon Jane. "Well, I am glad you've come. What is your name?"

"My name is—Jane," replied that individual, drawing a deep breath. The "Aubrey-Blythe" refused to be uttered.

"And I am Mrs. Belknap," graciously returned the young woman, apparently paying no heed to the omission. "I do hope," she added plaintively, "that Mary's sister hasn't been taken suddenly ill again. Mary has so many relatives, and they are nearly always ill—or dead."

Jane looked her astonishment.

"Mary is perfectly devoted to her family," Mrs. Belknap went on, "and that is really why I am hiring another girl. Mr. Belknap says I *must* have somebody to fall back upon when Mary is away. Can you cook?"

"Why, no, madam," said Jane stiffly. "I understood that I was to be a nursery governess, or parlor maid. Mrs. Streeter didn't seem to understand exactly."

"Why, of course, I shall want you to help me look after Buster," chimed in Mrs. Belknap, with a somewhat offended air, "and wait at table, and answer the bell, and do the sweeping and dusting, and the cooking and dish washing on Mondays and Tuesdays—regular second work, you know. Mary is really an excellent servant—when she's here. But now that she's out she may not come back for three or four days. If it wasn't so nearly impossible to get a good cook out here I should have changed long ago. But we're so near New York. I dare say, though, I shall get along very well now that I've got you."

The young man had turned his broad back on the two, and now strolled out of the kitchen with an air of extreme unconcern which ruffled Jane's temper afresh.

Her new mistress had disburdened herself of several parcels. "If you'll bring these upstairs for me," she said pleasantly, "I'll show you how to dress Buster—this the *third* time to-day—then I'll help you with the dinner. Of course, Mary may come back. But I'm afraid not. She hasn't been out for nearly a week, and I suppose she took advantage of my being in town."

Mrs. Belknap sighed profoundly, and Jane gathered up the parcels with a hesitating air. Unknown ills loomed very large at the present moment.

"Oh, by the way, did you bring your working clothes?" Mrs. Belknap wanted to know. She paused, with one foot on the stairs, for Jane's answer.

"Yes, madam; that is, I brought a black frock and some white aprons."

Jane's proud little head was flung back haughtily.

"And caps? You've no objections to a cap, I hope, because I shall require you to wear one. I bought some sweet little frilled ones to-day. I want you to put one right on. There's one thing more, I'm sorry I haven't two rooms for servants; but this house is so small, you see it's impossible. You won't mind rooming with Mary; she's very good-natured—as a rule. If you'll just come upstairs to the attic floor, I'll show you the way. Mary isn't so very neat about her room, though she's a splendid cook and laundress, and *so willing*—when she's here. Oh, dear! this is worse than I thought. Mary is so careless about opening her windows!"

Mrs. Belknap tip-toed daintily across the floor and flung the two windows wide. Then she turned a dismayed face upon Jane. "Mary isn't so very orderly," she repeated, rather vaguely. "But"—briskly—"now that you're here I do hope you'll try and keep this room in better order. That's always a second girl's work."

"What is a 'second girl,' if you please?" asked Jane. "I'm afraid I couldn't——"

"Oh, *don't* say that!" implored Mrs. Belknap hastily. "I'll explain about the work later. You won't find it hard. We're a small family, only myself and husband, and little boy—*only one child*—and my brother, Mr. Everett, is staying with us for a while."

"I couldn't sleep in this room, Mrs. Belknap," said Jane, in a low voice. Her eyes said plainly "I will not."

Mrs. Belknap fetched a deep, dispirited sigh. "I could put a cot in the trunkroom, I suppose," she said. "But, just for the present, won't you change your dress and— Oh, yes, we haven't spoken of wages or days out; have we? I was so upset to find Mary gone and Buster in such a mess. I'll tell you all about that later. I'll make everything satisfactory. But you see, I must hurry and get dinner started. I'm afraid the range fire is out, and Mr. Belknap will be at home at six. Please come down as soon as you can."

Jane relented a little at the tone of entreaty in the young woman's voice. "She's very young to be keeping house," she told herself wisely, as she invested her trim little figure in the black housemaid's gown with white cuffs and collar, which she had purchased at Mrs. Streeter's suggestion. "And she's certainly very odd in her manners toward a servant. But then, she's an American."

When at last she made her way to the kitchen Jane found her young mistress in a neat shirt waist and short skirt actively engaged in preparing a meal. Mrs. Belknap appeared to know exactly what to do, and in a miraculously short time had vegetables cooking, a salad in course of preparation, and a steak neatly trimmed and ready for broiling.

"Won't you set the table, Jane? You'll find the linen in the sideboard and the silver, too. Then put the plates to warm and a medium-sized platter and two vegetable dishes. I see Mary had the decency to leave a custard ready, and there's plenty of fruit."

As Jane awkwardly spread the cloth, and rummaged in the drawers for the required silver, she heard Mrs. Belknap's distinct American voice in the kitchen: "—not a bit of good, I'm *awfully* afraid, Jack,—afraid of doing anything, I could see that at a glance—Yes, one of those 'high-class servants.' *Pretty?* No, I don't think so—not at all. I'm surprised at you, Jack! I fear she's only one more in the long list of failures. Oh, *dear*, I'd give anything for a real *good* girl! It does seem——"

Jane guiltily opened the door. "Did you say I should lay the table for four, ma'am?" she asked.

"No, indeed; Buster will eat first, and he's almost starved, too, poor little darling! Yes, sweetheart, mother's hurrying. Jane, won't you take his bread and milk and this soft egg, and feed him at that little side table in the dining room? Or, no—" as the youngster vociferated his displeasure at this arrangement. "Do you want mother to feed you, darling? Carry him in the other room, please, Jack, and I'll come and feed him. Do you think you can broil this steak, Jane, and mash the potatoes?"

"I'll try, ma'am," said Jane coldly; "but I don't know anything at all about cooking."

"You don't? Why, how extraordinary!" exclaimed Mrs. Belknap suspiciously. "I should think you would know enough to broil a steak and mash potatoes, even if you have always been a parlor maid or a nursery governess. Do you think you can coax Buster to eat his supper?"

"I'll try, ma'am," repeated Jane; "but of course I'm a stranger to—Master Buster."

"Well, I think if you will try to look pleasant, and if you'll not be quite so *wooden* in your manner that he'll not dislike you. He likes almost everybody. If Buster doesn't like you, you will be of very little use to *me*."

Mrs. Belknap spoke in a tone of crisp decision which betrayed her rapidly growing conviction that Jane would not "do."

Jane divined this, and it piqued her pride, already sorely wounded. She walked into the dining room, with her pretty head held very high indeed, to encounter Mr. John Everett's blue eyes fixed upon her with an expression of respectful sympathy. He had thoughtfully installed his small nephew in a tall highchair, and was awkwardly tying a bib about his neck.

"I'm to feed Master Buster, if you please, sir," said Jane, with a severe tightening of her pretty lips.

"All right," agreed Mr. Everett cheerfully. "Now Buster, if you'll be a good boy and eat your supper without howling for your mother, I'll go down to the grocery store and buy you some candy. Do you hear, young man?"

"Yeth," assented the infant, fixing solemn, expectant eyes upon Jane. "Will you bwing her some, too?"

Apparently Mr. Everett did not hear this question. "Now, mind, Buster," he said seriously, "no kicking, no howling for mother. Sit up; be a man, and eat this supper like a Trojan. I'll be back before you're through, with at least four chocolate drops."

Jane sternly suppressed the feeling of gratitude, which threatened to well up in her homesick heart, with an exuberance entirely disproportionate to the occasion. But John Everett had already caught the upward flicker of the girl's long lashes, and the shadow of a smile which hovered about her mouth. This particular young American was thinking of many things as he strode briskly toward the grocery; but chiefly of the arena presented by his sister's small kitchen, and of the varied actors therein.

"Man's inhumanity to man may be a live topic," reflected Mr. Everett sagely, "but what about woman's inhumanity to woman? And yet sis doesn't mean to be unkind."

CHAPTER VIII

The growing conviction of her own folly haunted Jane even in her belated dreams, in which she found herself once more in the pleasant English schoolroom superintending her two small cousins in their youthful efforts to comprehend the fundamental principles of good conduct. "You should always be considerate to those beneath you, Percy," she seemed to be saying, "and help them whenever you can." Then she had quoted the grand old motto of the French aristocracy, "*noblesse oblige*," explaining how one's superiority in any particular only added to one's obligation to those less fortunate.

It was hard to awaken from this dream to find the rain beating heavily upon the roof of Mrs. Belknap's trunkroom, and to realize, from an inspection of the loud-voiced nickel clock which she had been told to take upstairs, that she was very late indeed.

Mrs. Belknap was engaged in preparing breakfast as expeditiously as was possible with her child hanging about her skirts and clamoring for his food. She bestowed an impatient glance upon Jane as she entered the kitchen, which had the effect of dispelling that young person's contrition as effectually as one of Lady Agatha's ill-timed reproaches.

"I am sorry to be late," said Jane stiffly.

Mrs. Belknap did not reply. At the moment she was adding boiling water to the coffee pot, and stirring its contents with a long-handled spoon.

Jane shrugged her shoulders. "She's an ill-bred person," she told herself resentfully. "Shall I lay the table, madam?" she ventured, after an uncomfortable silence, during which she watched her young mistress's deft motions with dismayed interest.

"That is already done," replied Mrs. Belknap, turning her pretty, flushed face upon Jane. "I believe I told you last night that Mr. Belknap and Mr. Everett were obliged to leave for the city on the half-past seven car. You should have been down an hour ago. I never call a servant," she added severely.

Jane swallowed hard. Then *noblesse oblige* recurred to her mind. "You did tell me," she said, very gently, "and I am sorry I overslept. I will try not to do that again. Shall I give Master Buster his breakfast, ma'am?"

A variety of expressions passed in rapid succession over Mrs. Belknap's mobile face, astonishment, pleasure, and a subdued twinkle of fun shone in her eyes as she again turned to Jane. "Why, yes; you may—if he will go with you."

A fleeting sense of wonder at this unchanging attitude of subserviency toward the infant pervaded Jane's English mind. Then she stooped toward the child. "If you will come with me, Master Buster, I will give you your breakfast."

The child stared at her thoughtfully; then to his mother's manifest astonishment he accepted the invitation. "I will do wiv oo," he said, with immense condescension.

Mrs. Belknap heaved a thankful sigh. "How *sweet* of the darling!" she murmured. "Here is his breakfast food, Jane. He likes it with cream and sugar. You may give him the juice of half an orange and two slices of this whole wheat bread toasted, with butter. He will breakfast with us this morning."

As Jane, in her frilled cap and white apron, bearing a tray, entered the dining room she encountered Mr. John Everett. He looked at her inquiringly. "Good morning," he said cheerfully.

"Good morning, sir," replied Jane unsmilingly, then blushed angrily to find herself blushing. "He is very rude to notice a servant so particularly," she told herself. Then her curiosity got the better of her, and she stole a second glance at him. Mr. Everett was apparently quite absorbed in his paper at the moment, and Jane had ample opportunity to observe the fine, strong lines of his clean-shaven face. He was undeniably handsome, Jane was forced to admit, and he looked kind and sensible.

The small boy known as Buster now appeared, borne high aloft in his tall father's arms, and presently the entire family was seated at the table.

Jane hated herself anew as she waited by her mistress's chair to pass the cups of coffee on her little tray. Try as she would she could not rid herself of the vision of Lady Agatha's scornful eyes, while Reginald and Gwendolen seemed quietly to mock her from across the sea. In an interval of absence from the dining room, in quest of fresh toast, she caught a trill of low laughter; then Mrs. Belknap's carrying voice—"Really quite impressive, isn't she? But I fear she's bound to be more ornamental than useful."

Jane's indignant blushes betrayed her to at least one pair of eyes when she reëntered the dining room, and Mr. John Everett plainly looked his displeasure at his pretty sister, who was still exchanging smiles with her husband.

"How would *you* like it, sis?" Jane heard him ask pointedly, as the two men were putting on their coats in the front hall.

"How *do* I like it, you mean, Jack. Well, I only hope you'll find me alive tonight," Mrs. Belknap had replied. Then she came out airily to the kitchen, where Jane was awkwardly gathering the breakfast things preparatory to washing them.

"Now, Jane," said Mrs. Belknap, producing a leather-covered account book, with a pretty air of importance, "I must have a little talk with you. What is your full name, please?"

"Jane Evelyn Aubrey-Blythe," replied Jane distinctly. "My nobleness obliges me to be truthful and polite," she thought.

Mrs. Belknap was surveying her with an incredulous smile. "Not *really*?" she said. "You found that name in a novel, didn't you?"

"No, madam," said Jane coldly, "that is my full name."

"Where did you work before you came to me?" went on Mrs. Belknap, with a pause of her busy pencil.

Jane hesitated.

Mrs. Belknap's clear eyes demanded instant answer, somewhat after the manner of a magistrate conducting a legal examination. Master Belknap, who was leaning upon his mother's knee in a complacently postprandial state, also centered his direct gaze upon the girl's face.

"I—worked, that is, I was last employed by a—Mrs. Markle or—Madam Melbrun," faltered Jane, loudly clashing the cups in her confusion.

"Be careful not to break the china, Jane," advised Mrs. Belknap, with housewifely care. "In what capacity were you employed by this Mrs. or Madam—what was the name?"

"I don't know," confessed Jane, with desperate frankness. "She told me her name was Markle; afterwards she said it was Melbrun."

Mrs. Belknap shook her head, as she again glanced seriously at the name with which she had just headed the clear, new page in her book of accounts. "I cannot understand," she said strongly, "why people should lie about their names, or, indeed, about anything. It is so much more *sensible* to tell the truth. That is what I often tell Mary: '*Do* tell me the truth, Mary,' I say to her. But I fear she never does."

"What, never?" exclaimed Jane, unconsciously plagiarizing from a comic opera.

"It is a habit, I fear," said Mrs. Belknap in a depressed tone, "telling falsehoods, I mean; some persons tell them when they might just as well tell the truth, even from their own standpoint. Of course," she added hastily, "it is always *right* and *best* to tell the exact truth. I hope, Jane, that *you* are a *truthful* girl. You will get on much better with *me* if you are. Now what did you do for this person for whom you last worked?"

"I smuggled," said Jane shortly.

"You—*what?*"

"Smuggled," repeated Jane; "I smuggled lace—five thousand dollars worth, the man said. Mrs. Markle sewed it in my jacket between the lining and the outside. But they found it and took it away."

Mrs. Belknap looked actually frightened for a minute. "I—I don't believe it," she murmured weakly.

"I didn't know Mrs. Markle put the lace there," Jane went on firmly. "She gave me a beautiful fur coat to wear on the ship, and asked me to leave my jacket in her stateroom. She sewed the lace in the jacket during the voyage."

"You *look* like a truthful girl," mused Mrs. Belknap. "But— Then you have just come to America," she added shrewdly, "and you have no references, of course?"

"No, Mrs. Belknap; I have not," replied Jane, expecting no less than an instant dismissal after this damaging statement.

To her great surprise the lady closed her book with a slight shrug of her shapely shoulders. "The matter of wages we discussed last night," she said tentatively. "Now I am expecting Mrs. Whittaker to wash this morning; you will put the kitchen to rights as quickly as you can. And remember, Jane, that although you have no references I shall soon be able to find out just what sort of a girl you are. I am not easily deceived."

This improving conversation was interrupted by the arrival at the back door of a tall, thin, dyspeptic-looking person attired in a rusty black gown and a dispirited hat, both of which articles of attire had obviously seen better days.

"Good mornin', Mis' Belknap," began this individual, with a trenchant sniff, as she divested herself of her draggled black skirt, which was thus revealed as a sort of drop curtain concealing a scant gingham wrapper beneath, girt about the waist with a decent checkered apron.

Mrs. Belknap displayed her white teeth in a winning smile as she replied. "And this is my new maid, Jane Blythe," she added, indicating that young person with an affable gesture.

"My! you ain't tellin' me that Mary MacGrotty's left you?" exclaimed Mrs. Whittaker in a sympathizing tone; "as good an' kind as you've be'n to her! I sh'd think she'd be 'shamed to treat you so mean. As I says to m' 'usband this mornin', 'Mary MacGrotty,' I says, 'don't know when she's well off, a-livin' with that sweet young lady.'"

"I expect Mary back within a few days," Mrs. Belknap said guardedly. "She's away just now."

Mrs. Whittaker bent over the tubs with a deep, discouraged sigh. "M' back's mos' broke this mornin'," she observed, flapping a wet sheet on the board and lathering it freely with soap; "but what with five childern to work fer, an' m' 'usband out o' work since Christmas, it comes pretty hard on a body. Was you expectin' to stay right along?"

"Were you speaking to me?" asked Jane coldly.

Mrs. Whittaker cast a guarded glance about the kitchen. "She's gone; ain't she? She ain't plannin' to keep *two*, is she?"

Jane made no reply. Mrs. Whittaker gazed at her for a moment with her soapy arms akimbo. "You won't like it here," she said at last. "I c'n see that without ha'f lookin'. *She's turrible to work fur. I* couldn't stan' her—more'n fur a day now an' then. As I tell m' 'usband, I wasn't made to be bossed by nobody. I'm awful proud an' independent, an' *she* thinks she's the hull thing. I guess if she knew all 'at I know 'bout the goin's on in this 'ere kitchen she wouldn't be quite so uppity."

A light step at the door announced the hasty return of Mrs. Belknap; Mrs. Whittaker was discovered diligently rubbing, with a sad, but resigned, expression of countenance.

"I brought down this embroidered shirt-waist for you to wash, Mrs. Whittaker, and will you please be careful not to rub the embroidery on the board; it isn't much soiled, you see; a little of this white soap will be best for the flannels and for all these fine white things. By the way, you haven't put any of that washing powder into the water, have you? I buy that for the floors and tables; Mary thinks she can't get along without it. But it is very bad for the clothes."

Mrs. Whittaker received the garment in question with an air of lofty unconcern. "I wuz never known to put that nasty yellow stuff in m' clo'es," she said haughtily. "I sh'd think you'd know me well 'nough by this time to be sure o' that, Mis' Belknap. You don't need to worry about nothin' when *I'm* in the kitchen."

"I know you're very careful, Mrs. Whittaker," the young mistress of the house made haste to assure her.

"I 'ope she'll keep out the kitchen the rest of the day," Mrs. Whittaker observed acridly, as the door closed on Mrs. Belknap's retreating figure. "The

- 58 -

simple idee of *her* teaching *me* how to wash! No washin' powder, indeed! Well, I guess I ain't a-goin' to rub m' fingers to the bone fur her! That there white soap ain't worth shucks. But I'll take it 'ome with me; it'll do to wash the childern with."

Mrs. Whittaker sighed deeply as she crossed the floor with the cake of white soap. "I'll just leave it in m' pocket," she said. "Is there a drop of tea in that pot? No? Well, I'll make me a cup, I guess. My! I feel s' kind o' weak an' gone at the pit o' my stomick this mornin', as I wuz tellin' m' 'usband: 'I guess I'll have to take it 's easy 's I can to-day,' I says. An' 'e says, 'Do,' 'e says, 'an' come home 's early 's you can, Maria.' No; you won't be in this place long. You won't like it. Me an' Mary gits along pretty fair; but she won't stan' another girl around. Many's the time she's said so to me, right in this kitchen."

Jane hastily hung up the tea towels; her ears were burning under the loose waves of her hair.

"I'll help m'self to what I want to eat," Mrs. Whittaker was saying amiably; "I know where everythin' is, an' you don't need to stay 'round here on my account. If you was wantin' to change yer place when your week's out I know a real nice woman down the street 'at ain't got a girl. I promised her yeste'd'y 'at I'd inquire 'round. I'd like to 'commodate *her*; her youngest girl's clo'es just fits my Edie May. She's a nice woman to work for, too; she ain't always a-snoopin' 'round like some other folks I know of."

Mrs. Whittaker paused to empty a liberal shower of the tabooed washing compound into the boiler which was beginning to steam upon the range; then she rummaged in the pocket of her gown with an abstracted air. "Gracious! I 'ope I didn't leave that washin' soda to home. No; 'ere it is."

Jane observed Mrs. Whittaker's movements with astonished interest as she proceeded to cast certain large fragments of a whitish substance after the washing powder. "Washin' soda's m' best friend, as I tell my 'usband frequent. I most always carry some with me. Most the women I work for can't abide it; but it takes the dirt out, an' it saves m' back. I don't ask 'em to buy it, an' 's long 's I furnish it m'self I say it's none o' their business. Mind, you don't say nothin' to *her* 'bout my puttin' washin' soda in the boiler! But I guess you ain't that kind nohow, as I was sayin'——"

Jane hurriedly fled, the woman's whining voice sounding in her ears.

CHAPTER IX

"Now, Jane," Mrs. Belknap observed pleasantly, "you may put the chambers and bathroom in nice order; and then you may sweep the stairs, the hall, and the front piazza. As a rule I should like to have all that attended to before breakfast. When Mary returns I will prepare a schedule of your work carefully arranged for the different days, so that there can be no possible misunderstanding with regard to it. Aren't you feeling well?" she added, with severe kindness, as she eyed Jane's proud little face which too plainly betrayed the wakeful hours of the previous night and the heavy, unrefreshing slumber of the early morning. "I hope you are not delicate."

Jane straightened her slim figure. "Thank you, Mrs. Belknap, I am feeling quite well," she replied coldly.

"Very well, then; you will find the brushes and dusters in this closet, and I should like you to be careful to keep them in their place.—Dear me! I wonder what that child can be doing?"

The sound of running water and the tinkle of broken glass reached their ears from an adjoining room. "Oh, you *naughty* boy! What *will* mother do with you!"

"I was dest cweanin' my teef, muzzer, an' I dwopped 'e' gwass, an' it *b-w-owke*!" explained the small boy earnestly. "An' all 'e' toof-powder 'pilled on 'e' floor! It's nice an' *s-w-e-et*, muzzer! I like toof-powder."

"Oh, Buster Belknap, you haven't been *eating* tooth-powder?"

"I cweaned my teef, an I dwopped 'e' gwass, an' I——"

Further explanations were rendered impossible by Mrs. Belknap's prompt and heroic measures. The naughty pink mouth was forced open and rapidly explored by maternal eyes and fingers, while Jane was required to fetch in rapid succession a glass of water, a clean towel, and a fresh pinafore.

During the process the small boy screamed and struggled manfully if ineffectually; but once washed, dried, and freshly arrayed he pranced gayly away, his countenance composed and cheerful.

Jane was by this time busily engaged in sweeping the front stairs, while she wondered miserably if any girl in the whole world could be so unhappy and friendless as herself. She wished gloomily that she had not run away from Portland Square. She condemned herself bitterly for the pride and vainglory of her hasty actions, and with it all wave after wave of desperate homesickness surged over her young soul. It was scarcely to be wondered at that dust accumulated in dark nooks and corners should escape the notice of the tear-blurred hazel eyes, nor that the unswept rugs should be thoughtlessly pushed to one side.

She was suddenly recalled to a sense of these shortcomings by Mrs. Belknap's crisp, American voice. "Why, *Jane*! You are not doing this work at all properly. One would think it was your first experience in sweeping!"

"It is, ma'am," said Jane hopelessly.

"Dear me! I'm afraid this will never do," went on Mrs. Belknap, with a discouraged sigh. "Can't you *see* the dirt? Here, let me show you!"

Jane stared at the faultless demonstration of housewifely skill with sullen resentment. In her own eyes she seemed to have sunken to a plane infinitely beneath that occupied by Susan, the housemaid in the Portland Square mansion. Susan, at least, knew how to do her work thoroughly and well.

"Now, Jane, will you try again?" asked Mrs. Belknap, pleasantly conscious of a most praiseworthy patience and self-control. "I am sure you can sweep down these stairs properly, *if you try*, and if you will put your mind upon what you are doing. Then these rugs—I *think* I told you to take them out of doors to brush. They are quite filled with dust and germs, I dare say."

Mrs. Belknap appeared to expect some sort of reply to this serious arraignment, for she eyed Jane searchingly.

"You didn't mention the rugs, ma'am," said poor Jane, with an uncontrollable quiver of her mutinous mouth; "but I will take them out, if you would like me to."

As she bore her burden through the kitchen Mrs. Whittaker suspended her monotonous labors to remark: "My! *I* wouldn't stir a foot to clean them rugs, if I was you. That's man's work. Mis' Radford—her 'at I was tellin' you wanted a girl—hires a man to clean the rugs every Thursday. 'Tain't no more'n right, neither!"

The sun was shining cheerfully out of doors, and a brisk wind was hurrying the big, white clouds across the April sky. In spite of herself the clean, wholesome air and active exercise restored Jane's spirits. "I'll soon earn enough money to pay my passage back to England," she told herself, "and then—I can easily get a place as governess somewhere."

The capricious breeze whipped her brown hair in clouds across her eyes, quite blinding her to the approach of the stout, rubicund, showily dressed person who paused to stare curiously at Jane before entering the kitchen door.

This individual was discovered in close consultation with Mrs. Whittaker as Jane passed through the kitchen.

"That's what I tol' 'er," the laundress was remarking plaintively, as she passed a succession of dripping articles through the wringer, "Mary won't never stan' another girl in 'er kitchen, I says, an' it'll likely lose me a day a week besides. It ain't right to take the bread out o' my pore childern's mouths to put into hern; that it ain't!"

Mrs. Belknap was investing her child in coat and cap, with a somewhat worried expression on her pretty face, as Jane reëntered the hall. "Please don't talk to Mrs. Whittaker any more than you can help, Jane," she said seriously. "I think it hinders her in her work."

"I haven't spoken to the woman, ma'am," replied Jane, justly indignant. "I can't help it if she talks to me; but I'm sure I'm not interested in what she says."

"You shouldn't answer me in that tone, Jane," advised Mrs. Belknap warmly. "Oh, I do believe Mary has come back!"

"Yis, mum; I've come back; but I ain't sure as I'll stay," announced a rich Irish voice from the door.

"O *Mary*! where have you been? I didn't know what to think when I found you were gone again."

"Well, mum, you hadn't no more'n turned the corner before the telephone bell rang. It was me cousin in Tompkinsville. 'O Mary MacGrotty,' she says, whin she heard my voice, 'Aunt Bridget's tuk awful bad,' she says; 'you must come to wanst!' 'I'll come,' I says, 'an' stay wid yez just *wan hour*! I've me dinner to get,' I says, 'an' me leddy's out.' But whin I got to me cousin's house I found me aunt in strong convulsions. 'Sure, an' you won't have the heart to lave 'er like this,' they all says to me; an' so I stayed the night. She's some better this mornin', the saints be praised; but I guess I'll be goin' back, as I see you've help a-plinty."

"O Mary!" Mrs. Belknap said earnestly, "I *want* you to *stay*. I've hired Jane to help me with Buster, and she'll wait at table besides and do the upstairs sweeping. You'll find it *much* easier."

Miss MacGrotty folded her fat arms and surveyed Jane with coldly critical eyes. "If I'd a known you was wantin' a sicond gurl, I cud 'a' got you my niece—me brother's youngest daughter, Annie. She's a *lovely* worker an' used to childern. Where did you git the loikes o' *her*," she added, with a scornful toss of her plumed head.

"From an agency in New York," replied Mrs. Belknap, with a conciliatory mildness of demeanor which astonished Jane. "I think you'll find Jane a pleasant help and companion, and Jane, I hope you'll get along nicely with Mary. And now that you've finished laying down the rugs, Jane, won't you put on your hat and go out with Buster. He's in the side yard; but I fear he'll run away if he's left to himself too long."

When Jane came down from her attic room attired for the street Mrs. Belknap stopped her to say pointedly: "You've forgotten your apron, Jane; you'll find a clean one in the top drawer of the dining-room closet."

Poor Jane was quite unaware of the subtle psychological processes which contributed to her feeling of loathing for that innocent and spotless article of attire. But the apron appeared to be the last straw added to the already intolerable burden of her acute discomfort. Her pretty face was clouded and gloomy as she walked slowly across the muddy road in pursuit of the brilliant red tam perched on Master Belknap's curly head.

Mrs. Belknap, watching from an upper window, frowned and shrugged her shoulders. "I don't know whether it will pay to bother with that girl," she murmured. "I'm sure I haven't experienced a peaceful moment since she came, so far; but perhaps I can train her if I am patient."

The training process presently called for a fresh rebuke, with copious explanatory notes and commentaries, when Jane returned to the house half an hour later bearing Master Belknap, who was screaming and kicking with all the pent-up energy of a young cyclone.

"What *is* the matter with Buster, Jane?" demanded his mother excitedly, as she ran hastily down the front stairs to receive the two.

"He wanted to play in the muddy water with another little boy named Buster Bliss," replied Jane, quite breathless with her exertions; "and when I asked him not to get wet, he threw mud at me and at the other child; then I thought best to bring him home."

"Oh, I don't like him to play with that Bliss child at all; he's a very rude boy!" exclaimed Mrs. Belknap. "I meant to have told you about that, Jane. Stop crying, darling, and let mother wipe your tears—poor little sweetheart; his hands are as cold as ice, and—why, Jane, his sleeves are wringing wet, and covered with mud; and his feet, too! dear, *dear*!"

"Yes, ma'am," said Jane, "he *would* play in the water; that is why I carried him home. He sat right down in the mud, ma'am."

"But why did you *allow* it? Really, Jane, I can see that you are not at all used to children. Have you ever had the care of one before? One has to *manage*, you know."

Jane made no reply. And Mrs. Belknap did not seem to notice the omission in the strenuous process of rehabilitation which immediately ensued.

Jane stood meekly by, supplying the needful articles one by one. When all was over and the child released from his mother's fond arms, with a rapturous kiss, she ventured upon a single question.

"When Master Buster says he 'won't' what am I to do, ma'am?"

Mrs. Belknap leaned back in her chair with a far-away look in her bright eyes. Finally she replied: "You must *contrive* not to have him say 'won't' to you, Jane. It requires infinite tact and patience to care for a high-spirited child like Buster. Of course, I could not allow you to *punish* him in any way. I do not believe in corporal punishment; and even if I approved of it, I should never relegate it to other hands."

"And about the other children, ma'am; I noticed several in the neighborhood while I was out. There was another very rude child named Buster Yates—at least the little girl who was with him said so—I couldn't help wondering——"

"About what, Jane?" asked Mrs. Belknap indulgently. "I suppose everything in America is quite new and strange to you," she added rather proudly; "I shall always be glad to explain what you do not understand."

"Would you mind telling me why so many little boys in America are called—*Buster*? It's a very curious name. I never heard it in England."

Mrs. Belknap laughed heartily. "That's very easily explained," she said. "It is really a nickname taken from a series of humorous pictures in one of the newspapers. Quite possibly people are overdoing it," she added meditatively.

Jane looked mystified.

"Our Buster's name is really Everett Livingstone, and the Bliss child is Ralph, I believe; and Mrs. Yates's little boy is named Frederick. The Caldwells call their Arthur 'Buster,' and in town the Elwells and the Farleys and—yes, ever so many others have 'Busters.' It must have struck you as being very singular."

"Yes, Mrs. Belknap," said Jane pointedly. "It did."

As John Everett was returning from the city that night, and many nights thereafter, he found himself dwelling with singular intentness on the piquant face of his sister's English maid; it seemed to look out at him wistfully from the damp folds of his evening paper, and to haunt the twilight seclusion of the ferryboat deck upon which he was accustomed to tramp many a breezy mile in his daily trips across New York's spacious harbor.

John Everett was a graduate of Yale and a budding lawyer, employed in a down-town law office. He had unhesitatingly expended every cent of a slender patrimony in obtaining his education, and at present was in the hopeful position of a strong swimmer striking out unhampered for a distant shore. He fully expected to reach that shore—some time; but a man swimming for his life in the deep and perilous current of an untried profession has no business to dwell upon the alluring vision of any woman's face. That the woman of his shy boyhood dreams was waiting for him on that far-off shore, he felt reasonably sure; but even this conviction could not prevent him from feeling sorry for Jane. She was struggling in deep water, too, and would she—could she reach the shore in safety, unless some one—

"I am a fool!" John Everett told himself vigorously, and squared his broad shoulders to the bracing ocean wind, which blew damp and salt from the vasty deeps outside the Hook.

Half an hour later he came upon Jane at the corner, whither she had been sent to post a letter. There were half-dried tears sparkling upon her long lashes, and her mouth drooped pathetically at the corners.

"What is the trouble, Jane?" he couldn't help asking; his blue eyes said more.

Jane ignored both. "There is nothing the matter, sir," she said icily, and drew back to let him pass.

CHAPTER X

More than a fortnight had passed and Jane was still engaged in "doing second work" in the modest detached villa, otherwise known as the residence of Mr. and Mrs. James Livingstone Belknap. Toward the end of her first week of service she had received a letter from her good friend, Bertha Forbes, urging her to return to England at once in the company of an acquaintance who was to be sent across on customhouse business. "I will arrange for the transportation," added Miss Forbes generously; "I want to feel that you are safe at home with your family once more."

Jane read this letter at the close of a peculiarly trying day, in which she had encountered divers rapids and cross currents in both kitchen and parlor. Mary MacGrotty was downright cross, Master Belknap peculiarly and aggravatingly mischievous, and Mrs. Belknap, grievously disappointed in her enlarged *ménage*, inclined to concentrate her irritation upon Jane's defenseless head.

"Sure, an' that gurl's more trouble than she's worth to ye," Mary MacGrotty had declared; "an' I towld yez when I come as how I c'u'dn't stan' fer no second gurl under me feet."

"If you weren't away so often, Mary," began Mrs. Belknap weakly, "I should——"

"Sure, an' I can't help *that*," interjected Miss MacGrotty strongly. "Blood is thicker 'an water, I'm thinkin', an' me fambly is that delicut an' ailin'. Me cousin's wife's mother was tuk bad of a Sunday," she added darkly. "I'm expectin' to hear of her death most any minute, an' the fun'ral 'll be to Brooklyn."

Mrs. Belknap sighed apprehensively. "By the way, Mary," she observed in a carefully modulated voice, which asked for information only, "have you chanced to see my carved shell comb anywhere about the house? I must have dropped it from my hair, I think, and I haven't been able to find it."

Mary MacGrotty faced about. "I have *not*!" she said emphatically. Then she pursed up her lips. "Hev you asked *her*, mum?" she demanded in a sepulchral whisper.

"You mean Jane? Oh, yes, I told her of my loss yesterday. Never mind; I dare say I shall find it soon. I hope so, anyway. It was rather a valuable comb, given me by Mr. Belknap soon after we were married, so I think a good deal of it."

Miss MacGrotty's red elbows vibrated slightly as her mistress left the kitchen; and Jane, who entered a moment later in quest of a glass of water for her young charge, found her smiling evilly into the depths of an iron pot.

"If you've got her comb hid away anywheres," muttered Mary, "you'd better watch out; she's onto yez!"

"But I haven't hidden her comb," retorted Jane, shaken out of her usual attitude of calm disdain toward the presiding genius of the kitchen. "You know I wouldn't do such a thing."

"Aw; do I, thin'!" jeered Miss MacGrotty. "Well, you moind what I say; that's all! *I* ain't a-goin' to be blamed fer your doin's, miss."

"I shall have to go back to England," Jane told herself, as she left the kitchen hot with rage and shame.

Master Belknap was for the moment playing peacefully in his sand pile, and Jane, who had been bidden to keep close watch upon his movements, stood looking down at him, winking fast to keep the angry tears from clouding her eyes. One, two, three great sparkling drops got the better of her and fell flashing into the sand; then Jane glanced up to find John Everett looking at her with an expression of poignant anxiety on his honest face.

"You are crying," he said in a low voice. "Why? Doesn't my sister——"

"Oh, it is nothing! I——" To her immense dismay Jane choked over an unmistakable sob which wrenched her slender throat. "I wish you would—not——"

"But I can't help it, when I see you so unhappy. Haven't you any friends in America?"

"No-o—that is—I have one," said Jane, remembering Bertha Forbes's unanswered letter.

"A man?" he asked, with sudden sharp anxiety.

Jane looked at him indignantly. "I don't know any man," she said.

"You know me," he murmured. "I should like to be your friend, Jane; may I?"

The girl made no reply. Instead she turned and walked steadily toward the house. "I will go back to England," she assured herself a second time. But when at last she had leisure to answer Miss Forbes's letter she found herself refusing her kind offer point blank. "I could not put myself under so great an obligation to you," she wrote. "Besides, I am quite safe and not too unhappy here; and I shall soon have earned the money for my passage."

Miss Forbes read this ingenuous epistle with a suspicious lifting of her sagacious brows. "I think I'll try and run over to Staten Island and see what sort of a place she's in," she said aloud.

But she forgot this friendly resolution in the rush of the next day's business, and was only recalled to the memory of it by an interview with one of the passengers on the incoming liner. The interview was not of an official nature, and its finish found Miss Forbes nervously chewing her pencil in a state of singular agitation.

To search for a person who has ostensibly started upon an indefinite tour of the United States is not unlike the traditional hunt for a needle in a haymow; nevertheless the Hon. Wipplinger Towle had gallantly embarked upon the quest, panoplied with infinite leisure, unlimited money, and the well-disciplined patience of middle age.

He had not seen fit to acquaint the house of Aubrey-Blythe with his intentions; being disposed, quite irrationally, to lay the fact of Jane's flight at its door. Mr. Towle was an exceedingly calm not to say mild-tempered man, a fact which very few persons intimidated by his stern eyes and boldly modeled chin ever found out; but upon occasions he could be severely implacable in his slowly acquired opinions. With a sagacity more than masculine he suspected that the failure of his matrimonial plans and the subsequent disappearance of Jane might be traced to Lady Agatha Aubrey-Blythe, and he actually had the temerity to tax that noble lady with both in her own drawing-room.

Lady Agatha's righteous indignation was kept in leash for some moments by her knowledge of Mr. Towle's wealth and the hope that his elderly fancy on matrimony bent might yet be guided toward the unattractive Gwendolen; but it burst its bonds when the full import of his deliberate utterances finally penetrated her intrenched understanding. She turned white with fury as she focused her light-blue stare upon the audacious Mr. Towle.

"Do you mean to *intimate* that you think it *my* fault that my husband's niece has *disgraced* herself and the family by running away like a governess in a cheap romance?" she demanded, in unequivocal English.

"Hum—ah," said Mr. Towle, quite unabashed. "I—er—beg your pardon, Lady Agatha, if I appear rude, but did you not say some rather nasty things to Jane the day before she left? I—er—fancy, don't you know, that it might make me run away to be told that I was absolutely unattractive, not at all clever, and—ah—dependent upon others for the bread that I ate."

"Did the shameless girl tell you that?" cried Lady Agatha, more enraged by the Honorable Wipplinger's uncompromising manner than by his words. "And after *all* that we have done for her, too!"

"Just—er—*what* have you done for her, if I may inquire?"

"What have we done for Jane Blythe? How can you ask such a question! The girl was left on our hands with scarcely a penny to her name when she was a mere infant. We have done everything—*everything*, and this is the way she rewards our kindness—our Christian charity! I trust I may never see the ungrateful creature again."

"If there is anything," said the Hon. Wipplinger Towle, with exceeding deliberation, "which I despise on earth, it is the—er—damnable sentiment miscalled Christian charity. It has ruined more persons than gin, in my humble opinion."

After which he took his leave with scant ceremony, Lady Agatha remaining stock still in her chair in a state of semipetrifaction.

An hour later, having recovered the power of speech, she requested her husband to formally forbid Mr. Towle the house; which Mr. Robert Aubrey-Blythe, on his part, flatly refused to do. Whereupon ensued one of an inconsiderable number of battles between the pair, during the course of which Lady Agatha, having taunted her husband with his inferior lineage, was reduced to tears by being reminded of her own dowerless condition when she condescended from her high estate to wed the rich commoner.

Perceiving his decisive victory, Mr. Robert Aubrey-Blythe waxed magnanimous to the point of begging the lady's pardon. "It's deucedly bad form to quarrel, Agatha; and what's more it's ruinous to the nerves and digestion," he had concluded sagely. "You've gone off ten years at least in your looks, my dear, from falling into such a rage over nothing at all."

"Nothing at all!" echoed Lady Agatha. "Why, Robert, the man used the most *frightful* language in my presence. Fancy being told that Christian charity has ruined more persons than gin! And as for the profane adjective he used in connection with that speech, I refuse to soil my tongue with it!"

Mr. Aubrey-Blythe cleared his throat with some violence. "Oh—er—as to that, I've always said that Towle was a clever fellow—a deucedly clever fellow," he observed meditatively. "He's nobody's fool, is Towle; and mind you forget all about this the next time I ask him to dine; for ask him I shall, Lady Agatha, whenever I please; and you'll be careful to be civil to him, madam."

But the Hon. Wipplinger Towle was not available as a dinner guest for several weeks thereafter; the fact being that having duly reflected upon the information conveyed to him by the grateful Susan, he had found that the shoe fitted, had instantly put it on, and had started for America on the trail of Jane.

Fate, as is her occasional custom, was scornfully kind to this elderly Sir Galahad, and he struck a warm scent before ever he had landed from the steamer in the shape of a romantic newspaper story in which figured an elderly French female smuggler, said to be an old hand at the game, and a beautiful and innocent young English girl (name not given). Scornful Fate glued the Honorable Wipplinger's eyes to this spirited account penned by an enthusiastic young reporter, who chanced to be nosing about the customhouse after material, and Mr. Towle, although as devoid of imagination as the average male Briton usually is, nevertheless pictured Jane as the unlucky heroine of the moving tale.

The reporter's richly adjectived phrase—"The slender little maiden, with her true English complexion of cream and roses, lit up by sparkling hazel eyes"—appeared to fit Jane with disconcerting completeness.

When he landed, immediately after perusing it, Mr. Towle took the pains at once to look into the matter; and this explains the unofficial interview before alluded to, in the course of which Miss Bertha Forbes reduced the top of her lead pencil to a splintery pulp, more after the fashion of an embarrassed schoolgirl than a stern-faced customs official.

"No, sir, we do not as a rule make it a practice to give out information regarding what takes place in our department," Miss Forbes informed the tall Englishman.

"Hum—ah; can you inform me whether there is any truth in this account?" Mr. Towle persisted. "The description of the—er—smugglers tallies with that of the two persons I am in search of."

Miss Forbes cast her eyes coldly over the newspaper item. "There have been several similar cases of late," she admitted. "But this states, you notice, that both parties were immediately dismissed upon confiscation of the goods. It is not a part of my work to keep track of detected smugglers, and so of course——"

"You—er—saw the young girl described in the story; did you not?"

"I—I couldn't be sure of it," prevaricated Miss Forbes, actually blushing.

The Hon. Wipplinger Towle fixed his glass more firmly in his eye and proceeded to stare the intrepid Bertha out of countenance "I beg your pardon," he observed masterfully, "but I—er—fancy you're mistaken."

"In what?" snapped the female inspector.

"In saying you're not sure you saw Miss Blythe. You—er—recall the whole incident perfectly, I am confident."

"Of all the—impudence!" murmured Miss Forbes, somewhat excitedly. "Well, suppose I do; what then?"

"If you know where she is, it will be greatly to her advantage if you will tell me," said Mr. Towle mildly.

"I don't know about that," mused Bertha Forbes. "Who, for example, are you? You're not her uncle."

"Thank you," said Mr. Towle astutely. "No; I am not a relative of Miss Blythe's. I am—er—merely a friend. But I beg to assure you that I have her best interests warmly at heart."

"Humph!—Well, I guess you have," admitted Miss Forbes, after a prolonged semi-official scrutiny of Mr. Towle's countenance, an ordeal which that honorable gentleman bore with the calm of conscious integrity. "But for all that I don't think I shall tell you where she is."

"Why not?" urged Mr. Towle, with an agitation which caused him to appear almost youthful.

"Because I'm sure she wouldn't thank me for it," said Bertha Forbes coolly. "Good day, sir."

"By heavens, madam, I'll not be put off like this!" declared Mr. Towle, very much in earnest. "I came to America on purpose to find her."

"Find her then," advised Miss Forbes, with tantalizing brevity. "I can't talk to you any longer to-day."

"To-morrow then?" Mr. Towle caught eagerly at the straw of suggestion in her last word.

But Miss Forbes was denied to unofficial visitors on the following day, and for three days thereafter, a period which Mr. Towle endured with such resignation as he could muster.

On the fourth day he intercepted that stony-hearted official on her way home to her lodgings. "Look here, Miss Forbes," he said doggedly, "I didn't offer you money the other day to tell me of Miss Blythe's whereabouts. But——"

"Don't do it to-day either," snapped the lady, with an ominous flash of her really fine eyes. "You're not in England, remember."

"Yet I find the cabbies and hotel people more rapacious than in London," Mr. Towle observed thoughtfully. "Nevertheless I beg your pardon, Miss—

er—Forbes, and I entreat you to tell me where Jane is. I—I believe I shall be ill if I can't find her."

"You *are* looking pretty well done up," acquiesced Miss Forbes; "but,"—seriously,—"how am I to be sure you are not the last person on earth she wants to see?"

"I wish to heavens I could be sure I'm not!" exclaimed Mr. Towle fervently. "But somebody ought to take her home."

"Granted," agreed Miss Forbes. "I've offered to send her back to England; but she won't go—for me. She might for you; but I doubt it."

"I have at least earned the right to try," he said, with something so convincing in his tone and manner that Bertha Forbes, who was at heart neither more nor less than a woman, surrendered at discretion.

"Very well; I'll give you her address, and you can go and see her, if you like," she said gruffly. "But I warn you she's an obstinate young person, quite bent upon having her own silly way."

CHAPTER XI

All of the foregoing took place on the same day that Mrs. Belknap wanted to know if Jane had seen her second-best gold hat pin. The day after that, three fine embroidered handkerchiefs were said to be missing from the little inlaid box on her bureau.

Mary MacGrotty displayed her big teeth in a malevolent smile when Jane rather fearfully mentioned this last circumstance in the kitchen. "You don't suppose the wind could have blown them away last Monday, do you, Mary? It was blowing hard, I remember," Jane said, nervously twisting her apron strings.

"It 'ud be a strong wind to lift 'em out the missus's box, I'm thinkin'," said Miss MacGrotty dryly. "But they wuz lifted, all right; an' no one knows ut better 'an you, Miss Innocence, wid yer purty face an' yer big saucer eyes."

Jane stared at the grinning Irish face, her own paling. "You are a bad, cruel woman!" she cried; "and you are not honest; I saw you take sugar out of the jar, and tea out of the caddy!"

Miss MacGrotty burst into a furious fit of coughing. "Aw, you impident little spalpeen, you!" she hissed, her face purple with rage. "Git out o' me kitchen this minute! We'll attind to your case prisintly. Yis, indade; I'll not have my character blackened by a light-fingered gurl from nobody knows where. Yis; you may stare, miss. You niver come honest by the foine rings in yer box, I'm thinkin', an' the little goold watch wid a di'mon' in the back, an' the locket wid pearls."

"You have been in my room!—looking at my things!" gasped Jane. "How dare you!"

"Git out o' me kitchen, or I'll tak' the procker to yez!" shouted Mary. "How dare I! Indade! Ye'll find it ain't best to gain the ill will o' Mary MacGrotty afore you're t'rough."

Jane went slowly up the stairs revolving many things in her mind. She was even considering the advisability of confiding her whole story to Mrs. Belknap, when that young matron's cold, even tones fell upon her ear.

"I wish to speak with you, Jane, for a moment," she said, with an air of severity, which stiffened Jane's pretty upper lip into haughty indifference.

"Yes, Mrs. Belknap," said the girl with a perfect propriety of manner, which aroused a wholly irrelevant resentment in the breast of the other woman.

"I wish to tell you, Jane, that last evening after you had retired a strange *man* came here—to the front door—inquiring for you. Mr. Belknap, who answered the bell, referred the matter to me, and I told him to say to the man that he could not see you."

Jane stared at her mistress in silence, indignation tempered with a certain speculative curiosity looking out of her bright eyes.

"He appeared"—Mrs. Belknap went on, with rising irritation—"quite like a gentleman. But *why* should a man—any man—come to my front door to inquire for *you*? I am sorry, Jane, but this circumstance, in connection with others, looks very suspicious to me. I do not *approve* of a girl in your situation attracting the attention of a man—more particularly of a man in a higher station of life. It is not at all proper; you ought to know that."

"Proper?" echoed Jane inquiringly.

"Perhaps I should have said *suitable*," amended Mrs. Belknap. "But I insist that you shall be quite truthful with me. Who was this man?"

"I'm sure I don't know, Mrs. Belknap," said Jane. "I don't know any men." Then she blushed guiltily.

Mrs. Belknap bristled with matronly dignity as she observed the girl's conscious face. "You may go now, Jane," she said, with an air of stern virtue. "But I wish to remind you once more that it is *always* best to tell the truth no matter how unpleasant the consequences may appear to you. If young girls in your situation in life could *only* learn that!"

Jane's eyes flickered and a shadowy dimple appeared at the corner of her mouth. "Suppose one does tell the truth, ma'am, and it sounds so queer that other people will not believe it?" she asked.

"That," said Mrs. Belknap, magnificently, "is not apt to occur. A sincere person can hardly be mistaken by another sincere person. And the *truth*, Jane, *never* sounds *queer*!" Which aphorism may be accepted for what it is worth.

The Hon. Wipplinger Towle, for the time being, had taken up his abode upon Staten Island, in a certain pretentious hotel which overlooks the bay, and quite undaunted by his reception of the previous evening he again presented himself at the street and number furnished him by Bertha Forbes. On this occasion the door was opened by Jane herself in cap and apron.

The mutual start of amazement which followed shook both man and maid out of the chill precincts of the conventionalities.

"My God—*Jane*!" exclaimed Mr. Towle. "What are you doing in this house?"

This pertinent inquiry brought Jane to herself with all the speed and thoroughness of a dash of cold water. "I am working for my living," she replied haughtily.

Mr. Towle stared helplessly at the girl. "I have come," he said at last, "to fetch you home."

"If you wish to talk to me," said Jane defiantly, "you will be obliged to come around to the back door. I will ask my mistress if I may speak with you in the kitchen for a few minutes. But there isn't any use of talking," she added. "I will not go home—at least not yet." Then she shut the door in his face.

Mr. Towle said something fierce under his breath; after which, without any hesitation whatever, he looked about for the kitchen entrance. "I'll talk with her," he said, "if I have to go to Hades to do it."

In the meanwhile Jane was interviewing her mistress. "Mr. Towle has come to see me, ma'am; may I speak with him in the kitchen for a few minutes?" she asked with haughty subservience. "Mary is out; and Master Belknap is playing in his sand pile."

Mrs. Belknap was in the act of putting the finishing touches to a dainty costume. She stopped short and faced about. "*Who* is Mr. Towle?" she demanded.

"He is a friend of—of Uncle Robert's, from England," replied Jane, rather sullenly to her mistress's thinking.

"Dear, *dear*!" murmured Mrs. Belknap, eying her pleasing reflection in the glass with a frown. "This is *too* much! And I was just on the point of going out to a reception; now, of course, I shall be obliged to——"

Jane looked up suddenly. "I don't wish to talk with him," she said.

"Then why not send him away? Wait! I will go down myself and speak with the man. I *hope* you haven't left him *alone* below stairs. There have been so many burglaries lately. He is in the kitchen, I suppose."

Jane smothered a hysterical laugh, as Mrs. Belknap's rustling skirts swept down the rear staircase. She heard her young mistress's distinct American voice in a tone of displeased surprise. Then a door closed sharply, and the girl heard a man's retreating steps passing beneath the open window.

"He must be horribly vexed," she murmured; "but I'll *not* go back to England." She did not choose to question herself too sharply as to her reasons for this dogged resolution. But she reflected that Mr. Towle appeared much older since she had last seen him.

Mrs. Belknap called her presently from below stairs. "I am going now, Jane; for I really must stop at Mrs. Brown's tea if only for a few minutes. But I shall not be away long. Keep your eye on Buster *every moment*; I am told there are gypsies about. And, Jane, if Mary isn't back by five you must open the draughts of the range and prepare the vegetables."

Left alone with her small charge, Jane sat down on the little green bench under the vines with a kitchen towel to hem. It was very quiet and peaceful, and the occasional distant roar of a passing trolley and the loud singing of a very fat red-breasted robin, which had its nest in one of the maples which were planted at stated intervals along the street, merely served to make the country stillness the more evident. Master Belknap was pleasantly absorbed in his endeavors to construct a two-foot mountain in the midst of the sand box, and apparently much entertained by the ceaseless action of the law of gravitation evidenced by the conduct of the unstable material at its apex. He did not look up at sound of the hasty steps which approached the house; but Jane did. Then she put down the brown towel with a displeased pucker of her white forehead.

"I thought that you had gone," she said coldly.

"I beg your pardon, but I wish to speak with that—er—young woman who dismissed me a half hour ago," said Mr. Towle, with exceeding politeness of manner. "I must see her. I wish to—er—explain. She was," he added thoughtfully, "an exceedingly rude person."

"If you are referring to Mrs. Belknap," Jane said, "I beg to inform you that she is my mistress; she sent you away with as little ceremony as possible for several reasons which it is not necessary for me to explain."

"Hum—ah!" murmured Mr. Towle. "Do you—er—mind telling me one of them?"

"Oh, if you insist!" said Jane, "I told Mrs. Belknap that I did not care to talk with you, and since she very particularly wished me to be at liberty to attend to my work, which is to look after her child, and to——"

Mr. Towle made a large gesture expressive of his extreme indifference to Mrs. Belknap's child and also her brown towel. "I came from England to find you, Jane," he said earnestly. "Why did you go away?"

"Why shouldn't I go away—if I chose?" Jane wanted to know, with a provoking drawl. She set two stitches in her brown towel with exceeding care, then put her pretty head on one side to survey the effect.

"There are at least two reasons why you should have stopped at home for every one you can give for running away," he said deliberately.

"But I didn't *run away*!" denied Jane crossly. "I—I just *went*. Aunt Agatha meant to send me somewhere because she hates me, I verily believe. I preferred to go."

"Nevertheless you should have stayed," he said gently. "Your position in life demanded patience and—er—pardon me—self-control. You exercised neither, it seems, and now—" His expressive look pointed the moral.

Jane winced under the prick of it. "How did you ever find me?" she asked, after a long pause filled with industrious stitching on the brown towel.

"I saw an account of the smuggling episode in an American newspaper," he said coolly. "Then, quite naturally, I looked up Miss Forbes at the customs department, and she gave me your address. It was surprisingly simple, you see, though it might easily have been far otherwise."

Jane bent her crimson face over her work. Her needle snapped in her trembling fingers. "I—I didn't know about that dreadful woman," she said in a low, shamed voice. "I supposed she was going to travel in America. How *could* I have known!"

Mr. Towle bent forward, his melancholy gray eyes filled with the warm light of pity and that deeper feeling to which it is said to be akin. "Poor little girl," he said in a deep voice, which fell upon Jane's ears like a caress. "You couldn't have known, of course. And I say it's all a beastly shame—the way they have treated you and all. Won't you let me take care of you after this, Jane? You shall never suffer so again."

Jane tried to answer; but somehow the words refused to come.

"Let me take you away from all this," he pleaded. "Won't you, dear?"

At this moment Master Belknap slowly climbed up the steps. "My neck is hot," he said seriously, "an' I want a dwink of water."

Jane arose with a sigh of relief. "Yes, Buster," she said eagerly. "I'll go and fetch it for you."

The little boy turned his clear eyes upon the man and studied him in silence for a minute. "Why did *you* come?" he said at length.

Mr. Towle looked down at the child with resignation. "If I should ask you the same question, my young man," he observed, "you wouldn't understand, I suppose. As a matter of fact, if you had—er—stayed away ten minutes longer, perhaps——"

"My Uncle Jack has a knife named after him," proceeded the child confidentially. "It is a Jack-knife. I yuve my Uncle Jack, an'—an' I yuve my Jane."

"Hum—ah," observed Mr. Towle. Then he removed his hat—for it was a warm day—and passed his handkerchief thoughtfully over the top of his bald head. Jane caught a fleeting glimpse of its dull, pale glisten as she paused with her hand on the latch of the screen door.

Her face, as she held the glass for the child to drink, was so severely grave and sweet that the Honorable Wipplinger's heart gave a sudden painful throb. "You haven't answered my question, Jane," he murmured, bending toward her.

She looked up at him with the merciless eyes of youth. "I really cannot do as you wish, Mr. Towle," she said slowly. "And—I must ask you to go away directly; I ought not to have talked with you here without Mrs. Belknap's permission."

"I can't leave you here in this false position," he said hoarsely. "For God's sake, Jane, listen to me! If you'll not marry me, let me take you home—back to England. This is no place for you."

Jane's pretty lips set in stubborn lines. "I shall stop here," she said, "until I have earned money enough to go back to England; then I shall find a—a position—somewhere."

She was leaning forward, her gaze riveted on the far end of the street. "And—and please go at once," she added breathlessly. "You must indeed."

The small boy had scampered across the weedy little lawn and climbed upon the fence. Now he hastily scrambled down and swung open the gate. "Uncle Jack!" he shouted; "I see my Uncle Jack. I'm doin' to meet my Uncle Jack; may I, Jane?"

Jane nodded.

"You really want me to go and leave you here?" the man said heavily. "Is it because——"

"If you care for me at all," she answered cruelly, "you would not wish to annoy me by stopping after I have asked you to go."

Halfway down the street he encountered a tall, athletic young man swinging easily along, the child perched upon his shoulder, his small hands buried in the man's thick waving brown hair. "Det up, Uncle Jack," shouted the boy gleefully, and drummed his small heels upon his bearer's broad chest.

Mr. Towle caught a fleeting glance of inquiry and half-humorous apology from a pair of honest blue eyes as the two passed on the narrow wooden sidewalk.

"You are a bally fool," groaned the Hon. Wipplinger Towle in his own ear, "and a cad to boot." And having thus frankly labeled his intentions, he deliberately turned to watch the tall young American, with his insolently handsome head, as he passed up the street and in at the gate of number 24 Vanderbilt Avenue.

"She must have seen him," muttered Mr. Towle, "before the boy did." Then he allowed the infrequent trolley car to slide past him into the sparsely settled country, while he tramped, his hat pulled low over his eyes, for many a dusty mile—how many he neither knew nor cared.

CHAPTER XII

When the Hon. Wipplinger Towle beheld the inhospitable shores of Staten Island fade into a dim haze of distance, which he accomplished from the depths of a comfortable steamer chair, placed in just the proper position on the deck of the newest Cunarder, it was without any rancor of soul or bitterness of spirit. He loved Jane Blythe as much (or more) than ever; but he was not disposed on that account to humiliate himself to the point of seeking stolen interviews with the object of his affection upon American back stoops. No; Jane must somehow be led to return to her native land, and once more in her proper environment, Mr. Towle could not find it in his heart to despair of finally winning her. He was a man of wide and varied experience, and he was not unaware that a period of discreet neglect upon his part might tend to enhance his apparent value.

It should be explained that during the course of that long and dusty tramp over the highways of Staten Island, whereon he had encountered clouds of bloodthirsty mosquitoes, the evidence of whose fierce attacks was even yet to be discerned upon his patrician countenance, the sagacious Mr. Towle had laid out a course of action from which he had not deviated an iota thus far, and in which his early return to England figured as a necessary step. In brief, he had taken the pains to satisfy himself that Jane Blythe's humiliating position was not in any sense an unsafe one, and that her sojourn under the roof of Mr. and Mrs. James Livingstone Belknap would result in little beyond what Mr. Towle was philosophically inclined to look upon as a needful though unpleasant experience. The only factor in the problem which really perplexed him was the presence of Mr. John Everett in the home of Mrs. Belknap. That arrogantly youthful figure suggested a possible painful finale to his own hopes, which Mr. Towle nevertheless found himself able to contemplate with resignation. He had arrived, in short, at that enviable stage of his experience when he had ceased to avidly desire what did not essentially belong to himself. "A man does not really want that which is another's," he was accustomed to say to the few intimates who were admitted to his confidence. "He only thinks or supposes that he does. The possession of it would make him as wretched as did the fabled black pudding which the unfortunate old woman acquired with the first of her three elfin-bestowed wishes. Made irrevocably fast to the end of her nose by her angry husband by means of the second wish, she was finally forced to rid herself of it by the sacrifice of the last and final wish."

Not that Jane Blythe ever appeared to Mr. Towle in the guise of a potential black pudding. He thought of her continually and sincerely as altogether good, lovely, and desirable; but as quite possibly too good, too lovely, and too desirable a possession for his lonely heart to selfishly appropriate. Something of this really chivalrous and exquisitely altruistic devotion was apparent even to the obtuse perceptions of Mr. Robert Aubrey-Blythe, whom Mr. Towle sought out immediately upon reaching London.

"I have found her, Robert," began Mr. Towle, without preamble.

"You have found——?"

"Jane," said Mr. Towle. The honorable gentleman did not appear at all excited, consequently Mr. Aubrey-Blythe, as in duty bound, sprang up from his chair, where he had been absorbed in a matter antipodally remote from the fortunes of his niece.

"Well, well, well!" cried Mr. Aubrey-Blythe excitedly, and "Upon my soul, Towle!" he said. "I *am* surprised!"

He was quite sincere in this statement, for beyond a few perfunctory efforts to trace the missing girl the Aubrey-Blythes had appeared piously resigned to the decree of a discerning Providence which had seen fit to remove so disturbing an element from their midst. Still it was annoying, not to say intolerable, to have one's acquaintances at the club and elsewhere preface their ordinary remarks with the query "Found your niece yet, Blythe?" or "Hear you've a deuced unhappy mystery to unravel at your house," with an occasional dubious reference to the morgue and the workhouse. So it was with genuine relief and pleasure that Mr. Aubrey-Blythe learned of the speedy and successful *dénouement* of Mr. Towle's foreign adventures.

"I am shocked and—er—grieved at what you tell me of the girl's present position," he added, with genuine mortification depicted upon his rotund countenance. "An *Aubrey-Blythe* in a *kitchen*—actually *working* with her *hands*! Preposterous, Towle, preposterous! I shall at once take steps to remove her."

"Hum—ah," murmured Mr. Towle; "better leave her where she is for a while longer."

"What is that you are saying?" inquired the other fussily. "No, no; that would never do, Towle—never in the world! Bless my soul; what will my wife, Lady Agatha Aubrey-Blythe, say to all this! Really, Towle, I dislike to disturb her ladyship with the shocking intelligence."

"I beg that you will not inform her of it," Mr. Towle said, rather sharply. "There is nothing to be gained by doing so, and much to be lost."

"The girl has never been a favorite with Lady Agatha," observed Mr. Aubrey-Blythe. "They seem to be—er—totally uncongenial."

"I can quite believe that," said the other dryly. He stared hard at his friend in silence for some minutes before he spoke again. "I believe you—er—informed me that your niece, Miss Jane Aubrey-Blythe, was— That is to say, you gave me to understand that she was entirely without fortune. Am I correct in this—er—particular?"

"And I," burst out Mr. Aubrey-Blythe, "understood you to say that the fact made no difference in your—ah— But, I beg your pardon, Towle; of course this—er—unfortunate escapade of the girl's ends all that—of course, of course! I shouldn't have spoken as I did."

"You misunderstand me, Robert," said Mr. Towle patiently. "My sentiments toward Miss Blythe are entirely unchanged; quite so, in fact. What I wished to say is this: I should like to settle some money on Miss Blythe, and—er—I don't know how to go about it. You must advise me, Robert."

"You would like to settle some money! Yes, I see; but this is no time to talk of marriage settlements, my dear fellow, with the girl in America, and———"

"I am not talking of marriage settlements," said Mr. Towle calmly. "There may never be a marriage between us; in fact I have scarcely any hope of it. I am too old, and"—with a slight bitterness of manner—"unluckily I look even older than I am. No; what I want is to give to Jane a comfortable sum of money outright, and leave her to be happy in her own way. If I can win her later on, I mean to do it fairly and squarely; but, as I have already said, I have very little hope of it."

"Gad, man! if you give the girl a fortune, she's bound to marry you; common gratitude, common decency, would demand it."

"Exactly so," quoth Mr. Towle. "But I'll have no common gratitude and common decency as you call it—and deuced common it is—mixing up in her feelings for me. Neither do I want her driven into a marriage with me as a *dernier ressort*. If she could—er—love me I— But never mind, Robert. We'll cut this short, if you please. And I don't intend, mark you, to give her a fortune; nothing that would attract a crowd of worthless fellows, you understand, but enough so that she may feel free and independent of—er—other people, including yourself, and be able to buy her own frocks and the feathers and frills that women love; a matter of ten or twelve thousand pounds, say."

"Very handsome of you, Towle, to have thought of it, I'm sure; uncommonly generous, by gad! but I doubt if it will be becoming in me to allow it. I fear that Lady Agatha———"

"You'll not tell her," interrupted Mr. Towle eagerly. Then he leaned forward and rested his hand upon the other's broad knee. "I'm not one to refer over often to the past, Robert, as you know; but I believe you've told me more than once that you—er—that I— No; I can't say it. It sticks in my throat."

"I know what you mean, Towle," growled Mr. Aubrey-Blythe. "There's no need for you to remind me that I'm under a tremendous obligation to you. But do you mean to tell me———"

"I declare to you that if you will help me to do what I wish in this one thing, I shall know the obligation to be on the other side. And, mind, it is to be kept a secret between you and me—forever."

Mr. Robert Aubrey-Blythe appeared plunged into profound meditation. At last he raised his head. "She wouldn't touch a penny of it, if she knew," he said at last. "Jane is deucedly independent and all that."

"She'd be obliged to take it if it came from a relative," suggested Mr. Towle; "couldn't you———"

The other shook his head. "Bless my soul, Towle," he murmured, with something very like a twinkle of humor in his eyes; "if I should attempt to settle a shilling piece on Jane there'd be the deuce and all to pay. I should think you'd know better than to suggest it."

"It's going to be done somehow, Robert," said Mr. Towle firmly, "if I—er—have to hang myself to bring it about. She couldn't refuse a legacy."

"Oh, I say; that would never do, Towle! You mustn't think of such a thing," protested Mr. Aubrey-Blythe, fidgeting in his chair. "But, speaking of a legacy, I wonder, now———"

He left his sentence suspended in midair, while he rummaged in his desk for a paper. "Hum—yes, yes. Now, I wonder— I—er—had a brother once, a younger brother, a sad rascal of a fellow, quite as improvident as poor Oliver—Jane's father, you know—and dissolute to boot. We don't often mention Foxhall Aubrey-Blythe, poor fellow; sad case, very. He's dead, in short. Died in South Africa a couple of months ago, without a sixpence to his name, as might have been expected. Now, I wonder— Of course, it would be very irregular and all that; but I fancy it could be arranged, with the help of a discreet attorney—eh? That is to say, if you won't think better of it, Towle."

"I should think it might be done," agreed the Hon. Wipplinger Towle seriously. "There can be no possible harm in it, certainly, to the dead man, or to anyone else. And it's got to be arranged, Robert. I'm quite set upon it."

After which the arch conspirators put their heads together over the details of a plot which, for the present at least, does not vitally concern the fortunes of Miss Jane Evelyn Aubrey-Blythe, who at that moment was industriously engaged in brushing the rugs, which she had carried out from Mrs. Belknap's little parlor to the untidy grass plot bristling with spent dandelion stalks, situated at the rear of the Belknap house.

Mary MacGrotty was clattering about the range inside the small kitchen, pausing to cast an occasional malevolent glance through the open window. Master Belknap was engaged in calmly propelling his tricycle up and down the sidewalk under the watchful eye of Mrs. Belknap, seated on the front porch with her sewing. It was an eminently peaceful domestic scene, which gave no sign of the volcanic possibilities lurking underneath the deceitful calm of its surface.

The seventh individual who was in process of being inextricably bound in the fast-spinning threads of a watchful Fate was Mr. John Everett, who sat in a certain Broadway office, ostensibly occupied with a very dry legal paper, whose intricacies he supposed himself to be diligently mastering. In reality this young gentleman was uncounted leagues away from the Broadway office, wandering in lands of faerie with Jane. Jane's eyes were bright and Jane's lips were red and tempting; Jane's little hands were clasped upon his arm as they two walked slowly (all in the land of faerie) across a velvet lawn, wherein neither plantain nor dandelion had ever encroached, toward a house—a little house, with balconies, perhaps, and dormer windows, certainly—Jack Everett couldn't be altogether sure of its outlines, since houses (in the land of faerie) have a way of changing while one looks, like dissolving lantern views. All of which was very much in the air and exceedingly foolish, as this worthy young man told himself sternly, when he found, at the expiration of half of a delightful hour, where he had really been spending his time.

CHAPTER XIII

Mr. Towle gave no sign of a continued interest in Jane's affairs; and because he did not, that imprudent young person felt herself to be lonely and neglected beyond her deserts. At night, in the stuffy seclusion of the trunkroom, she wept large tears into her thin pillow, and prayed with truly feminine inconsistency and fervor for numbers of things which she as resolutely thrust aside by day.

Twice she sought solace and advice from Bertha Forbes, and as often spurned both, when both were urged upon her.

"You remind me," said Miss Forbes at last, "of a horse we used to have out in the country. My brothers were burning the stumps out of a ten-acre wood lot one summer, and that animal *would* jump over the fence and go and roll in the hot coals and ashes whenever he got a chance till his hide was burned into holes. The creature must have suffered frightfully, but he persisted in doing it just the same. We had to tie him up after a bit."

"Oh, thanks!" cried Jane angrily, "perhaps you think I need tying up."

"I do, indeed," agreed Bertha Forbes cheerfully. She studied the pretty, wilful face in silence for a few moments. "You are much too fond of having your own way," she added sententiously, "and one's own way is so seldom the path of pleasantness that the Bible tells about. I know, for I've tried it."

She swallowed hard once or twice, then she went on in her gruffest voice. "Look here, Jane, I don't want to see you make the fool of yourself that I did. I somehow got the notion that a woman was just as able as a man to make her way in the world, and that I wasn't going to depend upon 'petticoat push' for my living. I despised the idea of being dependent upon anybody, and so I—I— Well, to cut a long story short, I told the only man who ever cared enough about me to want to take care of me, that I could take care of myself. I told him so three times in all, I remember. The third time he said, 'All right, Bertha; I reckon you'll have to try.' A year later he married one of those soft pink-and-white little things that I had always looked down upon as being too insignificant to despise. Yesterday——"

Bertha Forbes paused to gulp painfully once or twice. "Yesterday that woman passed me in her carriage. There was a child on either side of her, and she was dressed like a flower; which means, you know, a bit more magnificently than Solomon in all his glory. She didn't know me, of course. And I tramped on down to my office. You know what my work is, Jane."

"Yes, I know," and Jane blushed painfully. "I—I don't really like taking care of myself," she murmured, after a little, "but I can't see how I am going to help myself for a while. Anyway, you may be happier in your horrid office than that woman in her carriage, unless she—loves the man who gives it to her." The girl finished with a soft, far-away look in her brown eyes.

"Right you are!" cried Bertha Forbes, bringing down her capable-looking hand upon her knee with a businesslike whack. "I'm not envying the woman; not I. Fancy me with a ridiculous feather bobbing over one eye, and diamonds and folderols of all sorts disposed upon my person. Wouldn't I be a holy show?"

"You're really very good looking, when one looks at you carefully, Bertha," said the girl seriously, "but you need handsome clothes to bring out your good points."

"Guess my points good or bad will have to remain in innocuous desuetude then," Miss Forbes said gruffly. "'Nough said about B. F., my dear. And if you're set on staying on in your servile position, and allowing that absurdly pretentious little matron and her infant to walk all over you, I've nothing to say, of course. Do the men treat you properly, child?"

Jane stared at her friend resentfully. "I don't know what you mean," she said. "Mrs. Belknap's husband and brother are both gentlemen, and I—am her servant."

"That's all right, child; but mind you keep that good-looking chap—what's his name? Oh, Everett—yes; mind you keep him at his distance, whatever you do."

"*Bertha!*" cried Jane.

"You needn't 'Bertha' me," said Miss Forbes severely. "I'm an old maid all right; but I know a thing or two if I am forty, and now that Mr. Towle has gone back to England——"

"Has he gone back?"

"Well; why not? You didn't want him to stay on in America, did you?"

"N-o," faltered Jane, "I-I'm glad he's gone." Nevertheless she felt a more poignant throb of loneliness than usual as she stepped down from the trolley car in the gathering twilight at the close of her "afternoon out." Had it fallen to the lot of the Hon. Wipplinger Towle to present himself at that moment Fortune might have been genuinely kind instead of amusedly scornful in view of his aspirations.

That same evening Mrs. Belknap shut her chamber door safely after a careful reconnaissance of the hall. "Jimmy, dear, I'm *almost* distracted," she confided to her husband.

"Why, what's the matter, dear girl?" he asked, "has Buster been up to his tricks again? Or is Mary's cousin's wife's mother's brother 'tuk bad wid cramps'?"

Mrs. Belknap heaved a deep sigh as she shook her head; her pretty white forehead was puckered into unbecoming folds of deep anxiety. "*It's Jane*," she said in a sepulchral whisper.

"If you don't like the girl, get rid of her," advised Mr. Belknap strongly. "I've thought all along this two-maid business is a mistake for us. It's too—er—complicated, somehow."

"Oh, Jimmy Belknap!" exclaimed his wife reproachfully; "it was you who advised me to get another girl. You simply made me do it; you know you did. Mary is away so often, and——"

"Bounce Mary, too!" cried the perfidious Mr. Belknap cheerfully. "Let's have a new deal all the way 'round, Margaret. That Mary's a fraud, or I'm a duffer."

"Oh, but, Jimmy, she's such a good cook! And I'm sure I couldn't get another like her. Why, poor Mrs. Bliss hasn't had a girl these last two months, and she tells me she's tried *everywhere*! And the people across the street are alone, too, and——"

"*I* can cook," put in Mr. Belknap confidently. "You just let me get the breakfast. When I put my mind to it there's nothing I can't do about a house."

"Oh, *you*!" scoffed his wife, reaching up to pull a lock of wavy hair on Mr. Belknap's tall head. "After you've gotten breakfast, Jimmy, it takes me all the morning to put the kitchen to rights again."

"But my coffee is out of sight," pursued Mr. Belknap complacently, "and my poached eggs can't be beat. I believe,"—boldly,—"I could make a pie!"

"Of course you could," agreed his wife ironically, "but I shouldn't want to be obliged to eat it. But, seriously, Jimmy, I'm *losing* things—almost every day some little thing. Do you suppose it's *Jane*?"

Mr. Belknap looked grave. "It's more likely to be Mary," he said. "Perhaps," he added hopefully, "it's Buster. He's a regular magpie. Do you remember about my slippers?"

Both parents paused to indulge in reminiscent laughter over the memory of the missing slippers which had been found, after days of fruitless searching, in the spare bedroom under the pillows.

"He was helping me pick up—the blessed lamb!" said Mrs. Belknap fondly. "But I'm sure he hasn't picked up my shell comb, two hat pins, half a dozen handkerchiefs, my best white silk stockings, and your college fraternity badge."

Mr. Belknap whistled sharply. "What?" he exclaimed, "has my frat pin disappeared? I say, Margaret, that looks serious!"

"It was in my jewel box," went on Mrs. Belknap solemnly, "pinned carefully onto the lining of the cover. You know I scarcely ever wear it now; I'm saving it for Buster. But I happened to go to the box for something else the other day; and, Jimmy, it's gone!"

Mr. Belknap fidgeted uneasily in his chair. "Confound it!" he murmured. "Well, Margaret, I'd advise you to get rid of both of 'em; and meanwhile lock up your valuables. We can take our meals out for a while, if worse comes to worst."

"I hate to think it's Jane," sighed Mrs. Belknap; "she seems such a nice girl. But appearances are so often deceptive; I really ought to have *insisted* upon references."

"From the lady smuggler?" Mr. Belknap wanted to know.

His wife dissolved in helpless laughter. "I never believed that story for a minute," she said, "nor the Jane Evelyn Aubrey-Blythe part, either. She simply wanted me to think that she wasn't an ordinary servant, poor thing. It would be dreadful to go drifting around the world, drudging first in one house and then in another; wouldn't it, Jimmy? I am sure I can't think what sort of a maid I should have been."

Mr. Belknap surveyed his wife smilingly. "You'd have got *me* all right, whatever you were doing," he assured her.

"Not *really*?"

"Sure! I never could have resisted those eyes, dear, nor that mouth—never in the world!" And Mr. Belknap illustrated his present susceptibility to the compelling charms of the features in question in a way which caused his pretty wife to laugh and blush, and assure him (fondly) that he was a foolish boy.

"Then you really think I would better give both the girls warning?" Mrs. Belknap asked rather faintly, visions of the empty kitchen with its manifold tasks rising fearfully in her mind.

"That's what I do when there's a bad snarl in the office," Mr. Belknap told her seriously. "A good clean breeze of discipline that sweeps everything before it is a mighty good thing at times. Let 'em go. We got along all right before we ever saw Mary MacGrotty or Jane hyphen-what-you-may-call-her, either; and we shall live all the peacefuller after they're gone."

"But the missing articles—don't you think I ought to make her give them back? Isn't it a bad thing for a young girl like Jane to think she can—be so wicked with impunity?"

"It isn't 'impunity,' as you call it, if she loses her place."

"Yes, Jimmy, it is. She could get a dozen other places to-morrow. People are so nearly frantic for help that they'll take anybody. Why, Mrs. De Puyster Jones actually told me that she *expected* to lose a certain amount every year. She says that it used to worry her terribly when she first began housekeeping; but now she just mentally adds it to the wages, and says nothing about it, if it isn't *too* outrageous."

Mr. Belknap laughed dubiously. "Why, I say, Margaret, that's what they call compounding felony, or mighty near it," he said slowly. "I don't believe I could stand for that sort of thing."

"Mrs. De Puyster Jones says that, of course, she hasn't a particle of self-respect left when it comes to servants," continued Mrs. Belknap feelingly. "But she's too delicate to do her own work, and Mr. Jones won't board; so what *can* she do? What can *I* do?"

Mr. Belknap softly whistled a popular coon song as he walked about the room. Then of a sudden and with entire irrelevance he broke into loud and cheerful singing:

"Oh, I may be cra-a-zy!

But I ain't no—fool!"

CHAPTER XIV

John Everett sat before the fire in his sister's cheerful little parlor for a full half hour without uttering a word. He was thinking particularly and persistently of Jane, of her proud, sensitive little face beneath its cloud of curling dark hair, of her shy, haughty eyes which refused to meet his own, of her curving mouth which so often quivered like a child's on the brink of heart-breaking sobs. He wished that he knew more of the girl's history.

"Strange that Margaret takes so little interest in her," this altruistic young person said to himself impatiently, as he glanced across at his sister, who sat cuddling her sleepy baby in her lap in the warm glow of the fireside. Mrs. Belknap was talking and laughing gayly with her husband, who stretched his slippered feet to the cheerful blaze with an air of huge content.

This charming picture of domesticity, which he had so frequently admired and even envied in a vague, impersonal fashion, suddenly impressed Jack Everett as being little else than an exhibition of monstrous selfishness. What right had Margaret to sit there so radiantly happy and unconcerned while another woman, as fair and lovable as herself, shed lonely tears in her kitchen. It wasn't right, by Jove, it was not, he told himself hotly.

Just what provision did Margaret make for the amusement and recreation of her maids he wondered. His praiseworthy curiosity on this point presently got the better of his prudence. He arose deliberately and walked out into the kitchen.

Jane stood at the window gazing drearily into the darkness. She glanced about at the sound of his step, and he saw that her face was pale and that her eyes were brimming with large tears.

John Everett laid two magazines on the table. "I have brought you something to read, Jane," he said kindly. "This kitchen is a dull place of an evening; isn't it?"

Jane's homesick eyes wandered hopelessly about the clean, bare little place, with its straight-backed wooden chairs set primly against the painted wall, its polished range and well-scoured table, still damp and odorous with soap and water. A flamboyant advertisement of laundry soap and the loud-voiced nickel clock were the sole ornaments of the scene, which was illumined faintly by a small kerosene lamp.

"Thank you, sir," she said coldly; "but I have no time to read."

Her manner was inexorable, but John Everett saw that her little fingers were trembling. "Jane," he said softly, "I asked you once if I might be your friend. You did not answer me at that time. Have you thought about it since?"

"I did not need to think about it, sir. It is impossible."

"But why, Jane? Do you hate me?"

John Everett was doubtless quite unaware of the fervor and earnestness which he infused into these two short questions. There was much of the chevalier *sans peur et sans reproche* about this particular young American, and all the knightly enthusiasm and tender indignation of a singularly pure and impulsive nature had been deeply stirred at sight of the lonely and friendless English girl. He was, in short, compounded from the identical stuff out of which the Geraints and Sir Galahads and King Cophetuas of past ages were made, and so, quite naturally, he couldn't help saying and looking a great deal more than a modern young man ought to say and look under like circumstances.

Jane stared at him in resentful silence for a moment before she replied. "I know nothing of American ways," she said—which was not entirely true, by the way, since for years she had devoured everything she could lay her hands on concerning America—"but in England no gentleman would speak to a servant as you have spoken to me, unless——"

"Unless—what, Jane?" he urged.

"Unless he meant to—insult her," she said haughtily.

John Everett's handsome face flushed scarlet.

"Jane," he said sternly. "Look at me."

She raised her eyes to his reluctantly.

"Did you really think I was trying to insult you?"

"N—o," she faltered. "But——"

"In America," he went on eagerly, "there is nothing to prevent our being friends. Everyone works for a living here. There is no high and no low. In America a man who would wantonly insult a woman who works is not called a gentleman. He is called a scoundrel! And, Jane, whatever else I may be I am not a scoundrel."

A shadowy smile glimmered for an instant in Jane's clear eyes, and dimpled the corners of her serious mouth. Then she pierced his pretty sophistry with a question. "Does Mrs. Belknap know that you brought these magazines to me, and that you—wish to be my friend?"

"I shall tell her," he said firmly. "She will understand."

The girl shook her head. "Mrs. Belknap would be very much displeased," she said. "She would not like it if she knew I was talking to you now. She would think me very bold and unmannerly, I am sure. Indeed, as far as I can find out, being a servant in America is very like being a servant in England."

"Jane," he entreated, "tell me: were you ever a servant in England?"

She looked at him thoughtfully, as if half minded to take him into her confidence; then her eyes danced. "I was a nursery governess in my last place in England," she said. "And I left without a reference. Good night, sir, and thank you kindly for the books, but I don't care about reading them."

She dropped him an old-fashioned courtesy, with indescribable grace and spirit, and before he could gather his wits for another word had vanished up the dark stairway. He stood listening blankly to her little feet on the stair, and so Mrs. Belknap found him.

"Why, Jack!" she exclaimed; "what in the world are you doing in the kitchen? I heard voices and I thought perhaps Jane had a beau." Her eyes fell upon the gay-colored magazines which lay upon the table. "How did these come here?" she asked, a note of displeasure in her pleasant voice.

"I brought them to Jane," he said bluntly.

"To *Jane*? Why, Jack Everett! What did you do that for?"

"Why shouldn't I do it? The poor girl has nothing to amuse her in this beastly little kitchen. And I am sure she is quite as capable of enjoying good reading as anyone in the house."

"I gave the girls several of the old magazines only last week," Mrs. Belknap said with an offended lifting of her eyebrows, "and the very next morning I found Mary kindling the fire with them. I never knew a servant to appreciate really good reading. And *these*—well, all I have to say is that I hope you'll consult *me* the next time you wish to make a present to either of the maids. I fancy an occasional dollar would be in rather better taste, and quite in a line with what they would expect from you."

"Great heavens, Margaret! do you suppose I would offer money to *Jane*?"

"It certainly isn't necessary, Jack, for you to offer her anything; I pay her good wages," retorted Mrs. Belknap crisply. "I merely said that if you felt it your *duty* to give either of them anything, a dollar———"

Mr. Everett turned on his heel, very pointedly terminating the interview, and Mrs. Belknap went back to her fireside with a slightly worried expression clouding her pretty face.

"I wish Jack wouldn't be so perfectly absurd about poor people," she said discontentedly, as she curled up in a deep chair at her husband's side. "I don't mind his hobnobbing with the butcher and discussing socialism with the plumber, but when it comes to acting as purveyor of good literature for the kitchen, why it strikes me as being a little tiresome."

"What has our philanthropic young friend been doing now?" Mr. Belknap wanted to know.

"Presenting an offering of magazines to Jane in the kitchen. I declare, Jimmy, this is the last straw! I shall certainly dismiss the girl at the end of her month. I shan't do it before, though, because I have some shopping to do, and I must finish my sewing before I undertake the care of Buster again. *He* is devoted to Jane; poor little lamb!"

"Buster is a young person of excellent taste," murmured Mr. Belknap. "And so"—meditatively—"is Jack."

"Jimmy Belknap, what *do* you mean?" demanded his wife, with a nervous little clutch at his sleeve. "You don't *suppose*——"

Mr. Belknap chuckled. "Don't tempt a man so, Madge," he entreated; "it's so delightfully easy to get a rise out of you that I really can't resist it once in a while."

"Then you don't *think*——"

"My mind is an innocuous blank, dear," he assured her gravely. "I don't 'think,' 'mean' or 'suppose' anything which would give you a minute's uneasiness. I'll tell you what, Margaret, suppose we cut out both the girls, get our own breakfasts, take our dinners at Miss Pitman's, and then we can afford one of those dinky little runabouts. How would that strike you?"

"We'll do it!" exclaimed Mrs. Belknap rapturously.

Then these two happy people settled down to one of those periods of castle building in the air which young married lovers delight in, and upon whose airy foundations many a solid superstructure of after life is reared. And, being thus pleasantly engaged, neither of them gave another thought to the two young persons under their roof, both of whom, being alone and lonely, were thinking of each other with varying emotional intensity.

"I must find out more about her," John Everett was resolving. "Margaret appears incapable of appreciating her."

"I must be careful and not allow him to talk to me any more," Jane was deciding with equal firmness. "I can't help liking him a little, for he is the only person who has been kind to me in years." Which statement was, of course, eminently unfair to Mr. Robert Aubrey-Blythe, as well as to his noble consort, Lady Agatha, both of whom had repeatedly assured each other, within the past few weeks, that Jane had proved herself *most ungrateful* after all their kindness to her.

It is a singular fact that ingratitude thus persistently dwelt upon proves a most effectual palliative to one's natural anxieties concerning another. Lady Agatha, in particular, had found the practice of the greatest use of late. She had been able by means of it to dismiss all unpleasant reflections regarding her husband's niece, which might otherwise have arisen to disquiet her.

As for Jane, she seldom thought bitterly of Lady Agatha in the far country into which her rash pride and folly had brought her. Each day of her hated servitude brought the time of her deliverance and her return to England so much the nearer. Just what she meant to do when she got there she did not for the present choose to consider. From the little window of her attic chamber she could catch wide glimpses of the sea, which stretched vast and lonely between this strange new country and the land of her birth, for which she longed with the passionate regret of a homesick child. The shore itself was not far distant, and one of Jane's most agreeable duties thus far had been to convoy Master Belknap to the beach, where he delighted to dig in the warm sand.

The very next day after Jane's prudent rejection of John Everett's proffered friendship her mistress announced her intention of spending the day in town. "In the afternoon, Jane, you may take Buster to the beach," said Mrs. Belknap. "It will do the darling good. Be careful to watch him every minute, Jane, and do not allow him to play with other children," had been her parting injunction.

There were few persons to be seen when Jane and her little charge alighted from the trolley car. The yellow sand lay warm and glistening under the direct rays of the sun, and along the blue horizon drifted myriads of white sails and the vanishing smoke of steamers coming and going in this busiest of all waterways. Jane sat down in the sand with a sigh of happy relief, while Master Belknap fell industriously to work with a diminutive shovel.

"Jane!" he said earnestly, "Jane!"

"Yes, dear," said Jane absent-mindedly.

"I yuve 'oo, Jane! 'n'—'n' I'm doin' to dig a dreat big hole, an' 'nen—an' 'nen I'm doin' to build a dreat big house for 'oo, Jane!"

"Yes, dear," repeated Jane sweetly. The wind sweeping in across leagues of softly rolling waves brought a lovely color to the girl's face. She threw aside her hat and let the wild air blow the little curls about her forehead. It pleased her to imagine that the fresh, salty savor carried with it a hint of blossoming hedgerows and the faint bitter fragrance of primroses abloom in distant English woods.

The little boy trotted away with his tiny red pail in quest of clam shells; Jane followed him lazily, with her dreaming eyes. Then she sprang to her feet, the color deepening in her cheeks at sight of the tall, broad-shouldered figure which was approaching them at a leisurely pace. Master Belknap had dropped his shovel and pail, and was running across the sand as fast as his short legs could carry him.

"Uncle Jack! Uncle Jack!" he shouted gleefully. "Here we are, Uncle Jack! I digged a—dreat—big hole, an'—an', Uncle Jack, I'm doin' to build a dreat big house—all for my Jane!"

CHAPTER XV

John Everett answered the carping question in Jane's eyes with gay composure. "I promised Buster yesterday that I would come home early and join him at the beach," he said coolly. "I want to have a hand in digging that hole, myself," he added, rescuing the abandoned shovel from a sandy entombment.

Jane surveyed him gravely. "If you are going to be here all the afternoon," she said, "perhaps you will not mind if I go home. There are windows to clean, and I am sure Mrs. Belknap would not mind my leaving Master Buster in your care, sir."

His crestfallen face afforded the girl a transient amusement as she walked across the sand in quest of her hat. But Fate, in the small person of the infant, happily intervened as she was firmly inserting her hat pins and otherwise preening herself for hasty flight.

"Where 'oo doin', Jane?" he demanded imperiously.

"I am going home," replied Jane, with a conciliatory smile. "Mr. Everett will stay with you, dear."

"No!" murmured the sagacious infant, laying hold of the girl's gown with a determined hand. "N-o-o!" The last word ended in a loud wail of protest.

Jane flushed uncomfortably under John Everett's observant eyes, as she stooped to gently disengage herself. "I must go, dear," she repeated. "I have some work to do at home."

The child responded by throwing both chubby arms about her neck and wailing discordantly in her ear.

"Come, come, Buster!" exclaimed his uncle wrathfully; "you can stop that howling. Jane won't leave you. I'll take myself off instead, as I see I am decidedly out of it."

The small boy instantly relaxed his hold upon the girl and flew to his uncle. "No-o!" he shouted. "I want my Jane, an'—an' I want 'oo, Uncle Jack!" He clambered up his accommodating relative's trouser leg, and was assisted to a triumphant perch upon that young gentleman's broad shoulder, where he beamed upon Jane with innocent delight. "I yuve my Uncle Jack," he announced conclusively, "and I yuve my Jane!"

"That's all right, young fellow, and a proper sentiment too," murmured John Everett. Then he cast a pleading look at Jane. "Why persist in spoiling a good time?" he asked. "I'll play in the sand like a good boy, and I promise you I won't teach Buster any bad words, nor throw wet sand on his clean frock."

Jane's pretty face was a study. "Very well, sir," she said coldly. "It is not for me to say, I suppose." Then she sat down at a safe distance from the hole in the sand—in which the small diplomat, satisfied with the result of his *coup*, immediately resumed operations—and fixed her eyes on the sail-haunted horizon. All the sense of happy freedom which the wind had brought her from across the sea had suddenly vanished. She was gallingly conscious of the bonds of her servitude and of the occasional friendly glances which the big, pleasant-faced young fellow on the sand bestowed upon her.

"I hate him!" she told herself passionately. "If he knew who I was he would not dare call me 'Jane,' and smile at me in that insufferably familiar way. It is only because I am a *servant*. Oh, I *hate* him!" Her little hands clenched themselves till the nails almost pierced the tender palms, whereon divers hardened spots told of unaccustomed toil.

It was not an auspicious moment for John Everett to approach and utter a commonplace remark about a passing steamer. Nevertheless he did it, being anxious in his blundering masculine way to cheer this forlorn little exile, who he felt sure was in dire need of human sympathy.

Jane made no sort of reply, and after a doubtful pause he ventured to seat himself at her side. "That white tower on the farther side of the bay is one of the features of 'Dreamland,'" he observed. "At night one can see it for a long distance sparkling with electric lights."

Still no answer. He studied the girl's delicate profile in silence for a minute. "Wouldn't you like to see it sometime, Jane?" he asked.

She turned upon him suddenly. "How—how *dare* you—call me 'Jane,' and—and— Oh, I *hate* you!" Her kindling eyes scorched him for an instant, then before he could collect his scattered senses she burst into wild sobbing. "You wouldn't dare treat me so if I was at—at home," she went on between her sobs; "but you think because I am all alone here and—and working for wages that you—can amuse yourself with me. Oh, I wish you would go away and never speak to me again!"

His face had paled slowly. "I don't even know your name," he said quietly. "But I assure you, Miss—Jane, it has been very far from my mind to annoy you, or to———"

He stopped short and looked at her fixedly. "I must put myself right with you, Jane," he said at last. "You must listen to me."

Her low weeping suddenly ceased, and she lifted her proud little face all wet with angry tears to his. "I will listen," she said haughtily.

"I am afraid I don't altogether understand what you mean to accuse me of," he said, choosing his words carefully; "but I will tell you just why I have tried to make friends with you. I will admit that men in my station do not as a rule make friends with servant maids." He said this firmly and watched her wince under the words. "But, Jane, you are not at all like an ordinary servant. I saw that the first time I met you. I fancied that you had, somehow, stumbled out of your right place in the world, and I thought—very foolishly, no doubt—that I might help you to get back to it."

Jane's eyes kindled. "I can help myself to get back to it," she murmured, "and I will!"

"That is why I wished to help you," he went on, without paying heed to her interruption, "and I will confess to you that I came down here this afternoon on purpose to have a talk with you. I meant—" he paused to search her face gravely. "I meant to ask you to allow me to send you home to England."

"Oh, no—*no*!" she protested.

"Do you mean to remain in America, then?" he asked. "Are you satisfied with being a domestic servant?"

"No," she said doggedly. "I am going back when—when I have earned the money for my passage. I ought never to have come," she added bitterly. "I ought to have endured the ills I knew."

"Will you tell me what ills you were enduring in England?" he asked.

"I—I was living with relatives," she faltered, "and——"

"Were they unkind to you?"

"They didn't mean to be," acknowledged Jane. "I can see that now. But I fancied—I thought I should be happier if I were independent. So I——"

"You fell into trouble as soon as you stepped out of the safe shelter of your home," he finished for her. "You are right in thinking that you should never have come, and yet— Now won't you allow me to—advance the money for your passage? I assure you I shall be very businesslike about it. I shall expect you to return every penny of it. For I"—he paused to smile half humorously to himself—"I am a poor young man, Jane, and I have to work for my living."

She looked up into the strong, kind face he bent toward her. "I—thank you," she said slowly, "and I beg your pardon, too. I see now that you are—that you meant to be my friend."

"And you will accept my friendship?" he asked eagerly. "You will allow me to help you to return to England?"

She shook her head. "I could have borrowed the money from Bertha Forbes, if I had chosen to do it," she said. "She wanted to send me back at once. But"—with an obstinate tightening of her pretty lips—"I thought since I had gotten myself into this absurd plight by my own foolishness I ought to get myself out of it. And that is why I am working for wages in your sister's house. I shall soon have earned money enough to go home by second cabin; but I don't mind how I go, if only I go!"

Her eyes wandered away to the dim blue horizon which lay beyond "The Hook," and he saw her sensitive mouth quiver.

"Do you know you're showing a whole lot of splendid grit," he murmured appreciatively. "I know just how you feel."

"Now that I have told you all this," she went on hurriedly, her eyes returning from their wistful excursion seaward, "you will understand why I do not—why I cannot—" she blushed and faltered into silence.

"You really haven't told me very much after all," he said gravely. "Don't you think between friends, now, that——"

"But we are not friends," she interrupted him hastily. "That is just what I wished to say. I have explained to you that I have friends in England, and I have Miss Forbes besides. So there is no reason at all why you should give me or my affairs another thought, and I beg"—haughtily—"that you will not."

"O Jane! why?" he urged anxiously.

She cast an impatient glance at him. "You are so—stupid," she murmured resentfully. "But then you are an American, and I suppose you cannot help it."

He grimaced ruefully at this British taunt. "I fear I shall have to allow the damaging fact of my nationality," he said; "but I fail to understand how it is going to stand in the way of my thinking of you at intervals. If you knew more about Americans, Jane, you would see that it is mainly on that account I am bound to do it."

"You'll be obliged to keep your thoughts to yourself then," she told him, "for as long as I am in Mrs. Belknap's employ I am, undeniably, her servant and, hence, nothing to you. Do you understand? Because if you do not, I shall be obliged to find another situation at once."

"Oh, no; don't do that!" he protested. "Look here, Jane, I'm not quite such a duffer as you seem to think. I see your point, and I'll agree not to bother you after this. But I won't promise never to think of you again. On the contrary, I mean to think of you a great deal; may I, Jane?"

Jane arose. "It is quite time to be going home," she said coldly. "I must ask you not to speak to me again, Mr. Everett, and please come home on another car."

"But sometime, Jane, after this farce is played to its finis, don't you think———"

She turned her back upon him deliberately and walked away toward the trolley station, leading Master Belknap by the hand, meek and unresisting. During all this time the little boy had been contentedly laboring in the removal of sand from a hole of wide dimensions; his eyes were heavy with fatigue when the girl set him gently in his place on the homeward bound car. "I yuve 'oo, Jane," he murmured sweetly, laying his curly head in her lap. "I'm doin' to build 'oo a—dreat, big house!"

Five minutes later he was soundly asleep, and Jane, who had tried in vain to awaken him, was forced to lift his limp weight in her slender arms when the car finally stopped at her destination.

"Give the boy to me, Jane," said an authoritative voice at her side.

She looked up in real vexation. "I thought," she said reproachfully, "that you promised———"

"I promised not to bother you, Jane; but I didn't say I would never offer to help you again. Did you suppose for an instant that I would allow you to carry that boy up this hill?"

Jane crossed the street without a word, and speeding across lots, by way of a daisied meadow, reached the house first.

She was met at the door by her mistress. "Why, Jane, where is Buster?" inquired Mrs. Belknap anxiously.

"Master Buster went to sleep on the way home, ma'am," explained Jane, blushing guiltily, "and Mr. Everett, who chanced to be on the same car, kindly offered to bring him up the hill."

"Oh!" said Mr. Everett's sister, rather blankly.

CHAPTER XVI

Opportunity has been depicted as a sturdy youth, girded for swift flight, tapping lightly at one's door at uncertain intervals; then, when one opens as quickly as may be, more often than not showing but a pair of mischievous heels retreating into the mists of yesterdays—"Gone," we are told solemnly, "never to return!" A truer philosophy recognizes opportunity as the child of desire, and wholly dependent for continued existence upon its parent. So when opportunity comes a-knocking (as happens every day and wellnigh every hour of the day) let desire make haste to run and open to its child, knowing well that opportunity is but a weakling, and must be sheltered and nourished lest it perish with cold and hunger on the very threshold that gave it birth.

A lover, whether or no he be an acknowledged lover in his own eyes and in the eyes of his world, needs no teaching as to the relationship his eager desires bear to his fleeting opportunities. In his case, at least, opportunity obeys desire, as a child should ever obey its parent; and this, if the mad world would only pause to examine, is the chief reason why lovers are of all men happy.

All of which is submitted as a simple preamble to a simpler statement; *videlicet*: because John Everett wished to see and converse with the unconfessed object of his affections, he found ample opportunity to do so, and this despite the fact that Jane Blythe herself did not wish it. And here it should be observed that there is a wide disparity in the quality and character of desire. John Everett's desire to know Jane was natural, strong, vigorous, true. Jane's desire to keep the young man at a distance was—to put it in the form of a vulgar colloquialism—something of a fake. Therefore being a mere creature of straw it stood no sort of a chance against the bold, aggressive, opportunity-seeking wishes of John—as, indeed, it did not deserve. Fraud, even though it be a nice, modest, girlish, innocent little fraud like the one Jane was cherishing in her heart of hearts, should never be tolerated.

And so, although Jane frowned upon John on every suitable occasion, John the more determinedly smiled upon Jane, and she, being young and lovely and, after all, a mere woman, grew (quite stealthily) prettier and sweeter and more worthy to be smiled upon with every passing hour. And this despite the vinegar and gall which she was forced to mingle with her daily food partaken of in the Belknap kitchen under the glowering eyes of Mary MacGrotty.

But opportunity when worthily fathered and properly nourished, as has been noted, frequently grows into surprising stature and, moreover, develops aspects which astonish even its fondest well-wisher. It is at this point that

Providence, luck, fate—what you will—is apt to take a hand, and then—things happen.

The thirtieth day of May dawned clear and beautiful after a week of rain and cloudy weather, and Mrs. Belknap looking anxiously from her window in the early morning gave a girlish shout of joy. "What a glorious day for our ride with the Sloans in their new motor car!" she cried. "You haven't seen it, Jimmy; but it is the darlingest thing, all shiny and cushiony, with big lunch baskets on the side and a lovely, deep, horn arrangement that trails out behind on the breeze like an organ chord."

"The lunch baskets appeal to my most esthetic sensibilities," observed Jimmy blandly. "I suppose the organ chord arrangement is designed to distract the mind of the stationary public from the beastly smell of the thing. Did you say the kid was asked too?"

"Certainly Buster is going," said his wife. "Do you think for a moment I'd go off pleasuring and leave that blessed lamb at home all day? But"—lowering her voice—"Mrs. Sloan didn't invite Jack, and I'm *awfully worried*!"

"About what, dear? Jack won't mind; he can put in the day in any one of a dozen ways."

"Of course he *can*; but there's one way I don't want him to put it in."

"What do you mean, dear girl? Don't look so doleful! One would suppose you'd planned to spend the day in the cemetery."

"That's really the way one ought to spend it, I suppose," said Mrs. Belknap patriotically. She was still drawing her pretty brows together in a worried little frown; then she turned suddenly upon her husband. "You know what I said to you about Jack? I've been watching him, and I'm awfully afraid——"

Mr. Belknap was shaving, and at this unlucky instant he cut himself slightly. "Nonsense, Margaret!" he exclaimed in an appropriate tone of voice, "Jack doesn't need watching any more than I do; and if he did, it isn't your place to do it."

"Why, Jimmy Belknap, how can you say such an unkind thing! Am I not Jack's only sister? Of course I ought to care whether he is happy or not, and I——"

"He seems to be happy enough lately," hazarded Mr. Belknap, pausing to strop his razor with a slight access of irritation.

"That's exactly what I mean," put in his wife triumphantly; "don't you see, dear? Jack *does* seem happy, and that is why I am so uneasy."

"Do I understand you to say that as his only sister you wish to file a demurrer in the case? If so, I'll——"

"*Jimmy!*"

Mr. Belknap leaned forward and eyed his lathered countenance intently as he applied the glittering edge of his blade to his outstretched throat.

"It always makes me shiver to see you do that," breathed Mrs. Belknap; "if that horrid thing should slip! But as I was saying, Jimmy, I can't think how to manage about the girls to-day. It seems a pity to ask them to stay at home; though, of course, we shall be awfully hungry for dinner when we get home, and if Mary goes out, more than likely she'll not be back in time to get dinner at all. And as for Jane——"

"By all means let them both go out for the day, my dear; you've really no right to keep them in on a legal holiday. But I confess I don't follow your 'as I was saying'; you weren't saying a word about the servants. You were talking about Jack, and about Jack's being happy."

Mrs. Belknap looked justly offended. "If you would pay a little more attention to what I say to you, Jimmy, you wouldn't appear so stupid on occasions. No; I'll not explain further; you'd merely make it an excuse to tease, and very likely you'd report the whole conversation to Tom Sloan as a huge joke, and the two of you would roar over it; then I should be obliged to explain to Mrs. Sloan, and she's a perfect sieve. The whole affair would be all over town in no time, and that I simply could not endure."

"I'm safe this time, Margaret," he assured her solemnly; "for, honest Injin, I haven't a ghost of an idea as to what you're trying to get at!"

"I know what I'll do," cogitated his wife, waving him aside. "I'll manage it so that the girls shall leave the house a full hour before we do; they'll go to the city, of course. And I'll keep Jack here till we're off; by that time Jane will be well out of the way, and——"

"O *Jane!*"

"I see you are beginning to understand *now!*" said Mrs. Belknap; then she added plaintively, "I *wish* I'd *never* hired that girl, Jimmy!"

"I suppose there's very little use in asking why you persist in hanging on to her?" said Mr. Belknap.

"Don't you *see*, dear, it wouldn't do a bit of good to send her away now; indeed, I feel as if it were almost my *duty* to keep her." Mrs. Belknap said this with the resigned air of a martyr; and Mr. Belknap wisely forebore to make any comment upon the surprising statement.

*   *   *   *   *   *

It was delightfully fresh and breezy on the trolley car; and Jane on the front seat keenly enjoyed the noisy rush through the green, daisied fields and woods cool with shade and fragrant with wild flowers and young ferns. In the streets of the villages through which the car passed on its way to the ferry there was a brilliant flutter of flags, the unfamiliar stars and stripes looking strange and foreign in Jane's English eyes. Everywhere there were holiday crowds, little girls in white frocks and shoes, bearing wreaths and bunches of flowers; little boys in their best clothes with tiny flags in their buttonholes; women carrying babies, and men carrying lunch baskets, and other and bigger babies; showily dressed young girls with their beaux; besides a multitude of the unattached eagerly going somewhere. Jane felt herself to be very small and lonely and far from home in the midst of it all.

She had planned to spend her unexpected holiday with Bertha Forbes, and when at the end of her journey she was informed by Miss Forbes's landlady that Miss Forbes had departed to New Jersey for the day, she turned away with a feeling of disappointment which almost amounted to physical pain. What should she do? Where should she go, alone in the great unfamiliar city of New York?

There were numberless excursions by boat and train and flag-decked barges, and the throng of sightseers of every nationality jostled one another good-humoredly, as they surged to and fro under the hot sun in the narrow space at the terminals of the elevated and subway roads. Jane's sad, bewildered little face under the brim of her unfashionable hat attracted the attention of more than one passer-by, as she slowly made her way to the ferry ticket office. She was going directly back to Staten Island, with no better prospect in view then to pass the day alone on the back porch of Mrs. Belknap's house, when the might-have-been-expected unexpected happened; she came face to face with John Everett, cool and handsome in his light summer suit and Panama hat. The young man had evidently just landed from a Staten Island boat, and his grim face brightened as his eyes lit upon Jane, hastily attempting to conceal her small person behind a burly German woman bearing a bundle, a basket, and a brace of babies in her capacious arms.

"*Jane!*" exclaimed Mr. Everett; "how glad I am to have met you. Where were you going?"

"I am going back to Staten Island directly, sir."

"To do what?"

His eyes demanded nothing less than facts, and Jane, being characteristically unable to frame a successful fib on the spur of the moment, told the pitiful little truth.

"And so you were going back to stay all day on the outside of a locked house—eh? A cheerful holiday you'd put in!"

"I meant to take a long, pleasant walk, of course," amended Jane, "and——"

"Won't you take pity on me?" he pleaded. "I hadn't an idea how to spend the day, so I'd started with an aimless notion of fetching up at the country club and playing golf or tennis. But I don't care a nickel for either. You've never seen New York, Jane, and now's your chance. You'll be going back to England soon without ever having had a glimpse of this town, and that would be really foolish, since you're here; don't you see it would?"

Jane shook her head. "I—I couldn't," she hesitated; but her youthful eyes shone wistfully bright, as all unknown to herself she turned to cast a fleeting glance at the laughing holiday crowds pouring up to the elevated and down to the subway stations.

"Why, of course you can!" he said positively; and before she knew what had really happened she found herself, her weak objections overborne, seated in a flying train which looked down upon the gay panorama of New York's flag-decked streets.

"Where are—we going?" she asked him, and the little catch in her soft voice raised John Everett to a seventh heaven of unreasoning happiness.

"How would you like," he asked, "to let this train carry us the entire length of Manhattan Island—which is really the live heart of New York, you know—and bring up at Bronx Park? I was there once with Buster, and there are all sorts of queer birds and reptiles and animals to be seen, and a pretty winding river—we'll go up it in a rowboat, if you like the water; and we'll have our lunch in a little restaurant by the rocking stone, and then——"

"But—I'm obliged to be at home by five o'clock," she told him with a transient clouding of her bright eyes, "and—and I am afraid that Mrs. Belknap——"

"Jane," he began, in a low, persuasive voice, "just listen to me for a minute. You must have a reasonably independent character or you wouldn't be here in America. You remember what you told me the other day of how you came to leave your home in England; now that being the case, suppose you make up your mind to forget all about my excellent sister and her claims on you for just this one day and be yourself. Will you, Jane? It will be a lot more fun for both of us, and it won't hurt anybody in the world."

Jane drew a quick breath. "I'd like to," she said honestly.

At that very moment Mrs. Belknap, becomingly veiled and gowned and leaning back complacently against the luxurious cushions of Mrs. Sloan's new automobile, was saying to her hostess: "Oh, thank you so much for thinking to inquire after my brother! Yes, John is spending the day at the country club; he used to be a champion golf player—did you know it? and he enjoys a day on the links beyond anything." Then this sapient young matron permitted the carking cares of everyday life to trail away into the dust-laden distance with the mellow honking of the great horn—an experiment which Jane and John Everett were also trying to their mutual satisfaction on the sun-lit reaches of the Bronx River.

The boat which they hired at a rickety little landing stage was an unwieldy flat-iron shaped scow, designed with an eye to the safety of the inexperienced public as well as the profit of the owner; but Jane, bright-eyed and pink cheeked, seated in the big square stern, was not too far away from John on the rower's seat, and the unwieldy craft presently carried the two of them around a wooded bend, out of sight of a group of roystering picnickers on the bank, into a quiet nook where the tall trees looked down at their reflection in the lazily flowing water.

"It reminds me," said Jane with a sigh, "of England; there is a river like this near Uncle Robert's place in Kent, only it isn't muddy like this."

"One has to be far from home to really appreciate its strong points," he observed meditatively; "I never shall forget how I felt after nearly a year abroad when I came suddenly upon the American flag waving over a consulate building somewhere in Italy. I hadn't an idea up to that moment that I was particularly patriotic, and I'd been enjoying my trip immensely, but I could have fallen on the neck of the wizened little chap inside just because he was born in Schenectady, New York. But as a matter of fact, Jane, our rivers are not all muddy; you ought to travel about and see more of America before you allow yourself to form cast-iron opinions about it. You've seen nothing but our seamy side yet, and quite naturally you can't help setting America down as a very disagreeable place, and bunching all Americans as cads."

Jane's brilliant little face dimpled mischievously. "Oh, no, I don't," she said sweetly; "I have the highest possible esteem for Bertha Forbes. She is an American and a very superior person, I am sure."

"You mean by that, I suppose, that you think her fair-minded and kind-hearted; don't you?"

"I suppose I do," admitted Jane. "Bertha is clever, too, and amusing—sometimes."

"Nearly all Americans are clever and amusing, in spots," he said confidently, "and numbers of us can fill the rest of the bill clear down to the ground; you'll see, Jane, when you come to know us better."

She shook her head. "I am going back to England in June," she said, "and I never expect to come back."

"Do you mean that you never want to come back?"

Jane shrugged her shoulders slightly. "I might possibly return to travel about sometime," she admitted, her mind reverting to Mr. Towles's parting words. "I am very fond of travel."

"So am I," he said somewhat ruefully, "but I fear I'll not do much of it for some years to come."

Jane's eyes remained pensively fixed upon the opposite shore. She was apparently quite indifferent to Mr. Everett's future prospects, and after a short pause, which he devoted to a careful study of the girl's clear profile, he observed tentatively: "I hope you'll not lay it up against Margaret—the way she treats you and all, I mean. She's really an uncommonly good sort, when one comes to know her; but, of course, she can't—I mean she doesn't understand——"

"I thought we were to forget Mrs. Belknap for this one day?" murmured Jane, with a little curl of her pretty lips.

He flushed uncomfortably. "What I meant to say was this: it occurred to me that it might be advisable for you to make a clean breast of the whole thing; to—to tell Margaret all about yourself and how you came to leave England, and so put yourself right. I—I wish you would, Jane."

She fixed her clear eyes upon him thoughtfully. "It has occurred to me, too," she said; "but—there is really no need to say anything to Mrs. Belknap. I shall try to do my work as well as I can while I am in her house; after that,"—she paused, then went on deliberately—"I shall go away, and that will be the end of it."

He dipped his oars strongly. "It shall not be the end of it," he told himself determinedly. Aloud he said, with a fine show of indifference: "You will, of course, do as you like; but I am sure Margaret would be glad if you would take her into your confidence."

Jane smiled with a fine feminine understanding which was lost on the man. "It will be much better not, I am sure," she said sweetly.

CHAPTER XVII

As John Everett and Jane Blythe walked slowly along the shaded winding path from the rustic bridge where they landed from the flat-iron shaped scow, the girl was thoughtfully silent, and the man glancing at her averted face felt vaguely uncomfortable. But he could hardly have been expected to know that Jane's thoughts were perversely busying themselves with the Hon. Wipplinger Towle. She was wondering uneasily as to what that eminently correct Englishman would think at sight of her walking, quite alone and unchaperoned, with a man, as appeared to be the strange American custom. Then for perhaps the fiftieth time she speculated upon the singular abruptness with which Mr. Towle had abandoned his wooing after her final dismissal of him on Mrs. Belknap's back stoop.

"He might at least have sent me word that he was going back to England," she told herself with some indignation, "if he really cared for me as much as he says."

The thought of that dear, distant island of her birth colored her answer to John Everett's cursory remark concerning the buffaloes, which lolled in all their huge unwieldy bulk inside a trampled enclosure. "Awkward chaps; aren't they?" he observed; "but the Government is doing its best to preserve them at this late day. They used to be slaughtered by tens of thousands on the plains, you know, until they bade fair to become extinct."

Jane shrugged her slender shoulders indifferently. "They are like everything else I have seen in America," she said, "much too big and ugly to be interesting."

The tall American cast a laughing glance at the little figure at his side. "We've more room to grow big in than you have in your 'right little, tight little isle,'" he said pleasantly. "Now if you're half as hungry as I am, you're ready to become a generous patron of natural history to the extent of eating some lunch at this restaurant. The net proceeds of all these places of entertainment are said to be turned in to purchase more beasts, birds, and reptiles for the public delectation."

Jane blushed resentfully as they seated themselves at a small table in the restaurant which was little more than an exaggerated veranda, open on all sides to the fresh breeze, the sight of the neat waitresses, in their caps and aprons, reminding her poignantly of her own anomalous position. She glanced fearfully about, half expecting to meet the scornful eyes of some one of Mrs. Belknap's acquaintances to whom she had opened the door, and whose cards she had conveyed to her mistress upon the diminutive tray which Mrs. Belknap had lately purchased for that express purpose. There were other young women at other round tables, wearing astonishing gowns and preposterous picture hats, and attended by dapper young men in smart ready-made suits and brilliant neckties. Amid the pervasive hum of toneless American voices, pieced by occasional high-pitched giggles, Jane became painfully conscious that her own gown was old-fashioned and shabby to a degree, and in marked contrast to the trim elegance of her companion's garb.

His eyes, released from a study of the bill of fare, followed hers with a half humorous and wholly masculine misapprehension. "These are New York's working girls out for a holiday," he said, "and they've certainly got Solomon cinched, as the boys say, on attire; haven't they?"

"If they are working girls, they are very unsuitably dressed," Jane said primly. Then she glanced down at her own frock made over from one of Gwendolen's cast-offs by her own unskilled fingers, and sighed deeply.

"I like a—a plain gown best; one made of blue stuff, say, and not too—too much frilled and furbelowed," he observed, with a fatuous desire to ingratiate himself, which met with instant and well-deserved retribution.

"It isn't kind nor—nor even civil of you to say that," murmured Jane, in a low indignant voice; "I'm only a working girl myself; and as for my frock, I know it's old-fashioned and—and ugly. I made it myself out of an old one; but you needn't have looked at it in that—particular way, and——"

"Jane!" he protested, startled at the fire in her eyes and the passionate tremor in her voice, "I beg your pardon for speaking as I did; it wasn't good manners, and I deserve to be squelched for doing it. I don't know any more about gowns than most men, and yours may be old-fashioned, but it is certainly the most becoming one I have seen to-day!"

Jane gazed at him searchingly. Then her mouth relaxed in a shadowy smile of forgiveness.

"Ah, here's the luncheon at last," he cried, with an air of huge relief, "and I hope you're as well prepared to overlook probable deficiencies as I am."

There is something primal and indubitable in the mere act of partaking of food at the same table which has always served to break down intangible barriers of reserve. By the time Jane Blythe had eaten of the broiled mackerel and fried potatoes—the latter vegetables being of the color and texture of untanned leather—she felt better acquainted with the man who shared these delectable viands with her than she could have believed possible. And when the two of them had finally arrived at the point of attacking twin mounds of pink and white ice cream, vouched for by the smiling young person who waited on them as "fresh strawb'r'y an' vaniller," she was ready to laugh with him at the truly national ease and dispatch with which the loud-voiced, showily-dressed damsels in their immediate neighborhood were disposing of similar pink and white mounds.

And when after luncheon they followed the crowd to the lion house, Jane's brown eyes grew delightfully big at sight of the great beasts ramping up and down in their cages and roaring for their prey, which a blue-frocked man shoved in to them in the convenient shape of huge chunks of butcher's beef. From the spectacle of the great cats at food, the current of sightseers swept them along to the abode of the simians, where they found monkeys of all sizes, colors, and shapes, gathered from every tropical forest in the world, and bound always to arouse strange questionings in the minds of their nobler captors. Jane lingered before the tiny white-faced apes with the bright, plaintive eyes and withered skins of old, old women. "They seem so anxious," she said, "and so worried over their bits of food, which is sure to be given them by a power which they do not understand."

John Everett looked down at her with quick understanding of her unspoken thought. "They might better be jolly, and—so might we," he murmured. "I suppose, in a way, we're in a cage—being looked after."

"And yet we seem to be having our own way," Jane said.

After that she was ready to enjoy the ourangs, dressed in pinafores, and sitting up at a table devouring buns and milk with an astonishing display of simian good manners under the watchful eye and ready switch of their trainer. When one of these sad-eyed apes suddenly hurled the contents of his mug at his companion's head, then disappeared under the table, she laughed aloud, an irrepressible, rolicking, girlish peal.

"They make me think of Percy and Cecil at tea in the nursery at home," she explained; "they were always trying experiments with their bread and milk, and when they were particularly bad Aunt Agatha was sure to find it out, and scold me because I allowed it."

"I can't imagine you a very severe disciplinarian," he said, "though you do manage Buster with wonderful success."

He regretted the stupid allusion at sight of her quick blush, and made haste to draw her attention to the Canadian lynxes snarling and showing their tasseled ears amid the fastnesses of their rocky den.

Neither paid any heed to the shrill exclamation of surprise to which a stout person in a plaided costume surmounted by a lofty plumed hat gave vent as she recognized the slight figure in the blue serge gown. The stout lady was industriously engaged in consuming sweets out of a brown paper bag; but she suspended the half of a magenta-tinted confection in midair while she called her companion's attention to her discovery.

"I'll cross the two feet av me this minute if it ain't *hur*!" she cried.

Her escort, who was distinguished by a mottled complexion, a soiled white waistcoat, and a billy-cock hat tipped knowingly over one red eye, helped himself to a block of dubious taffy, as he inquired with trenchant brevity: "Who's hur?"

"An' bad 'cess to hur English imperance, if she ain't wid *him*!" went on the lady excitedly; "sure an' it's Mary MacGrotty as'll tell the missus what I seen wid me own two eyes come to-morry mornin'. An' whin I'm t'rough wid hur ye'll not be able to find the lavin's an' lashin's av *hur* on Staten Island! Aw, the young divil!"

Happily, the unconscious object of these ambiguous remarks moved on without turning her head, and was presently lost to view amid the shifting crowd.

There was much to be seen at every turn of the winding paths, and Jane's girlish laugh rang out more than once at the solemn antics of the brown bears, obviously greedy and expectant despite the official warnings against feeding the animals, which were posted everywhere; at the bellowings and contortions of the mild-eyed seals, as they dashed from side to side of their tank, or "galumphed" about on the rocks. It was Jane who supplied the missing word out of "Alice in Wonderland," and John declared that it was the only word to describe the actions of a seal on dry ground, and hence deserved an honorable place in the dictionary.

Neither of them noticed the lengthening shadows, nor the gradually thinning crowd, till Jane observed a pair of huge eagles settling themselves deliberately upon a branch in their cage. "They look," she said innocently, "as if they were going to roost."

Not till then did the infatuated John Everett bethink himself to glance at his watch.

"They *are* going to roost, Jane," he said soberly, "and we've a long trip before us."

Jane could never afterwards recall the memory of that homeward journey without a poignant throb of the dismay which overwhelmed her when she spied Mary MacGrotty's leering face in the crowd that waited in the ferryhouse. Miss MacGrotty's countenance was suggestively empurpled, and her gait was swaying and uncertain as she approached Jane.

"I seen yez wid *him* to th' Paark," she whispered, "ye desaitful young baggage!" Then she stepped back into the crowd and disappeared before the girl could collect her wits to reply.

Jane's pretty color had faded quite away, and her eyes looked big and frightened when John Everett joined her with the tickets. "Oh, if you please!" she whispered, "won't you let me go alone from here. I—I mustn't be seen—with you, sir."

The last piteous little word almost shook him from his self-control. "You have a perfect right to be seen with me, Jane," he said firmly; "and I will not leave you alone in this rough crowd; but if it will make you any more comfortable I will sit a little distance away—but where I can watch you, mind—once we are aboard."

Mrs. Belknap had reached home before them, and Master Buster, cross and tired, was handed over to Jane immediately upon her arrival. "I am very sorry to be so late," the girl said, with a shamed drooping of her head.

And Mrs. Belknap replied kindly: "You've not had many holidays since you've been with me, Jane; I hope you enjoyed this one."

"I—I did indeed," choked Jane; "but I ought—I must explain——"

"Not to-night, please; it really makes no difference for this once!" her mistress said crisply.

CHAPTER XVIII

Mrs. Belknap was brought up face to face with the inevitable by Mary MacGrotty, who presented herself the next morning in the door of her mistress's room. Miss MacGrotty's countenance was stern and gloomy. Her words were few and to the point.

"I ain't goin' to stay wid yez no longer," she said.

"Why, what can have happened, Mary?" Mrs. Belknap asked, with hypocritical solicitude.

Miss MacGrotty eyed her young mistress haughtily. "Sure, mum, an' you know well enough widout askin' me," she said. "There ain't no room in wan house for hur an' me."

"Do you mean Jane?"

"I do, mum; I mean Jane, wid her purty face an' her big eyes an' her foine goin's-on behind the back o' yez. It ain't fer me to worrit the life out o' yez wid tellin' you all 'at I know. But I'm sorry fer yez; that's all."

The inexperienced Mrs. Belknap fell into the artful trap with ease. "What do you mean, Mary?" she demanded anxiously.

Miss MacGrotty shrugged her shoulders. "I'll trouble yez for me money, mum," she said loftily. "I'll not make no trouble in the house."

Mrs. Belknap happily remembered her husband's counsel at this crucial moment. "Very well, Mary," she said coolly, "I will look over my account book and have the money ready for you when you have packed and put your room in order."

Miss MacGrotty threw back her head with a defiant toss. "Sure, an' I'll not be lavin' the house till I've had me rights! There's things been missed, an' I'll not have it said that Mary MacGrotty wud touch the lave of a pin!" Then of a sudden she melted into copious tears. "I've be'n that happy an' continted sinse I come to live wid you, Mis' Belknap; sure, I can't bear the thoughts of lavin' you an' Master Buster, wid the shwate little face on him. If it wasn't fer *hur* I'd never be thinkin' of goin'; but my feelin's has be'n hur-r-t an' trampled on till I can't bear it no more. Tell me *wan thing*, Mis' Belknap, wasn't we all goin' on peaceful an' happy loike before *she* come, wid Mis' Whittaker to wash an' sweep, an' me in the kitchen?"

Mrs. Belknap temporized weakly. "Do you mean to tell me that if I will discharge Jane, you will stay?" she said at last.

"I do, mum; an' may I cross my feet this day if I stay in the same house wid hur another week. She ain't my sort, mum!"

Still Mrs. Belknap hesitated. Jane was proving herself a most intelligent caretaker for the idolized Buster. Indeed his mother was forced to acknowledge that that young person's conduct showed a not inconspicuous improvement since he had been under the firm but gentle rule of English Jane. On the other hand, Mary's bread and rolls were faultless, her pastry and salads beyond criticism, and her laundry work exhibited a snowy whiteness and smoothness most gratifying to the eye and touch of a dainty woman like Mrs. Belknap; singularly enough, not a single MacGrotty relative had sickened or died since the advent of Jane.

This last reflection colored her next remark. "You have been much more reliable lately, Mary," she observed thoughtfully, "and we all like your cooking."

"*Reliable!*" echoed Miss MacGrotty warmly, "reliable? Ain't I always reliable? Why, mum, in the last place where I wuz workin' four years to the day, an' where I'd be yet on'y the leddy died—a shwate, purty leddy she wuz, too. Often's the toime I've said to meself, 'Mis' Belknap's the livin' image of hur,' I says, an' that's why I can't bear to be leavin' yez, mum. But, as I wuz sayin', Mis' Peterson she wud be sayin': 'Oh, Mary MacGrotty!' she says, 'I don't know what I'd be doin' widout *you*,' she says. 'You're *that reliable*,' she says. Of course, I've had turrible luck wid me family bein' tuk bad since I lived wid you. But, the saints be praised! they're all well an' hearty now, exceptin' me brother's youngest gurl that's bad wid her fut from bein' run over by a milk wagon. Yis, mum, a turrible accident, it wuz, mum. *Hev ye looked in hur things?*"

"Have *I what?*" faltered Mrs. Belknap.

"Looked in that gurl's trunk, mum," repeated Miss MacGrotty in a ghostly whisper. "If you ain't, you'd better; that's all."

"Oh, I shouldn't like to do that. Dear, *dear*! what ought I to do, anyway?"

"A workin' gurl what brags of havin' a goold watch wid a dimon' in the back, an' a locket wid pearls an' two goold rings, wan of 'em wid a foine blue stone in it, ain't honest, I sh'd say."

"Did Jane——?"

"I seen 'em wid me own eyes," affirmed Miss MacGrotty dramatically. "'Where did you git the loikes o' thim?' I says to 'er. 'They wuz giv to me,' she says, 'in me last place,' she says."

"Dear, dear!" repeated Mrs. Belknap. Then she straightened her trim figure. "You may go now, Mary; I shall be obliged to talk with Jane, and with Mr. Belknap, too. I don't wish to be unjust."

"You'd better talk to Mr. Everett, mum, whilst you're talkin'!" said Mary, with artful emphasis. "Sure, an' he's too foine a gintleman entirely to———"

"You may go to your work at once, Mary," repeated Mrs. Belknap sternly. "I will tell you to-morrow what I have decided to do." Nevertheless the last barbed arrow had found its mark in Mrs. Belknap's agitated bosom. "I wonder if Jack—could—" she murmured, her mind running rapidly back over the past weeks. He had taken the girl's part masterfully in the few half-laughing discussions which had taken place concerning the romantic fortunes of Jane. "She is a lady, sis," he had declared stoutly, "and you ought to treat her like one."

"Impossible!" she thought. Of course there couldn't be such a thing in America as the rigid class distinctions of England; still, an *Everett* could hardly be seriously attracted by a *servant*. It was, she decided, merely another case of dear old Jack's overflowing goodness and kindness of heart—a heart which seemed big enough to harbor and warm the whole world of forlorn humanity. It was, in short, "the Everett way." Margaret Belknap recalled her father's beautiful courtesy which had exhibited itself alike to the washerwoman and the wife of the millionaire. All women were sacred in the eyes of the Everett men. And a poor, sick, helpless or downtrodden woman was the object of their keenest solicitude.

Why, Jack, she remembered, had on one occasion carried Mrs. Whittaker's little girl through the mud and rain for a full block, with that melancholy personage following close at his heels, delivering fulsome panegyrics on his goodness. "And there wasn't a bit of use of it, either; the child could have walked perfectly well," Mrs. Belknap reminded herself. Jack was the dearest boy in the world—except Jimmy; but, of course, he was *absurd*—sometimes. All men were. It was her manifest duty to see to it that no appealingly helpless female succeeded in attaching him to her perpetual and sworn service. It was her duty; and she would do it.

This praiseworthy resolution shone keenly in her blue eyes when Jane encountered them next. Behind the resolution lurked a question. Jane answered it by asking another. "I fear you are not satisfied with my work, Mrs. Belknap," she said meekly. Somehow or other, without exactly knowing why, she had become increasingly solicitous about pleasing this pretty, clear-eyed young matron, who, it might have seemed, was not so difficult to please.

"Why, yes, Jane," Mrs. Belknap answered hesitatingly, "I *am* pleased with your work. You are really very neat about your sweeping and dusting, now that I have taught you how"—this with a complacent tilt of her brown head—"and you really manage surprisingly well with Buster. I think he positively likes you—*the darling*! But———"

Jane waited the outcome of that "but" with a sinking heart.

Mrs. Belknap was gazing at her hand-maiden's downcast, faintly blushing face with searching eyes. "Jane," she said at last, "Mary has given me warning."

"Do you mean that Mary is going to leave you, ma'am?"

Mrs. Belknap sighed involuntarily. "Yes; that is what I mean. I was so sorry, Jane, to hear from Mary that you two cannot live peaceably in the same house. And then——"

"What else did Mary say about me, Mrs. Belknap?" demanded Jane with kindling eyes.

"She said—. O Jane, how can I tell you? You *seem* such a nice girl!"

"I *seem*—yes, madam; but you think I am not what I seem. Well, I am not. I ought not to be doing the work of a servant in this house. I ought never to have come here." Jane threw back her pretty head and stared at Mrs. Belknap from under level lids.

Mrs. Belknap returned the look with one of startled interest. She had recalled the smuggling episode. "What—do you mean, Jane?" she asked. "You are not——"

"I am a lady," said English Jane haughtily; "and so I do not belong in anyone's servant's hall. That is what I mean."

"Oh!—*a lady*!" repeated Mrs. Belknap, and she smiled. "Everyone who works out in America is 'a lady.' We who employ servants are simply women. But perhaps you did not know that, Jane." She remembered her brother's emphatic assertions, and added kindly: "I have noticed Jane, that you appear somewhat above your station. But you should remember that honest work never hurts anyone's real character. Character is marred by—by something quite different. When one allows oneself to be tempted to—to take what belongs to another, for instance."

"Do you mean, Mrs. Belknap, that you think *I* stole the things you have missed?" demanded Jane, her hazel eyes darting fire. "Did that wicked Mary say *that* to you? Yes; I see that she did. And you"—with bitter anger and scorn quite impossible to convey—"believed it!"

Mrs. Belknap appeared to grow small in her chair under the direct light of the girl's indignant eyes. "I—I do not *accuse* you of anything," she faltered. "I wish above all things to be just to everybody concerned."

Jane was silent. She was thinking confusedly of *noblesse oblige*. "You told me you were not easily deceived," she said, after a long pause; "but you are. If you were not blind you would *know* that I am incapable of anything of the sort. But if you prefer to believe Mary because she cooks your food as you like it, I shall not complain. I cannot cook."

This random shaft hit so squarely in the bull's eye of Mrs. Belknap's wavering thought that for the moment that worthy young matron was quite overcome with confusion. Then she rallied her forces.

"Now that we have entered upon this very disagreeable conversation, Jane, we may as well come to a full understanding—if such a thing is possible," she said decidedly. "I dislike more than I can tell you mentioning the matter, because it would seem to be none of my affairs; but Mary told me that you had shown her several articles of jewelry which struck me as being—well, to say the least, as unsuited to a young girl situated as you seem to be in the world, and——"

"I never showed Mary anything that belonged to me, nor talked to her about myself," said Jane stonily. "But I will show the contents of my box to you, madam—if you have not already seen it," she added keenly.

"No—no, Jane, indeed, I have not!" denied her mistress. "I have never made a practice of looking into a servant's possessions without her knowledge, as so many housekeepers do." Mrs. Belknap was feeling thoroughly uncomfortable; quite, as she afterwards expressed it, as though she were the culprit brought to the verge of a damaging confession.

"Very well, madam, if you will come upstairs to my room with me I will show you my watch and my locket, and whatever else I have which you think may interest you."

The faint irony in Jane's well-modulated tones brought the color to Mrs. Belknap's forehead; but she arose determinedly. "Thank you, Jane," she said, "it will be best, I think."

Jane threw open the door of the metamorphosed trunkroom with the air of an empress. "Please sit down, Mrs. Belknap," she said politely. Then she opened the lid of her trunk. "This is my watch, of which Mary spoke to you. It belonged to my mother; it has her monogram on the back, you see; and inside is her name, Jane Evelyn Winston."

Mrs. Belknap's eyelids flickered inquiringly.

"Winston was my mother's name before she was married," Jane explained, with a scornful curl of her pretty lip. "This locket has my father's picture in it, as you see. Mother used to wear it on her neck. I can just remember it."

"It is a very handsome locket," murmured Mrs. Belknap.

"And these are mother's wedding and betrothal rings. This sapphire is very old; it belonged to my great-great-grandmother Aubrey-Blythe. There are some other jewels which belonged to mother, but Uncle Robert has them put away for me. I suppose I shall never see them again."

Jane choked a little over her last words, and two or three big, homesick tears dropped on the two rings.

"*Jane!*" exclaimed Mrs. Belknap, with sudden sharpness, "what—what is *that*?" She was pointing to a corner of the trunk, her eyes round with horrified surprise.

Jane's tear-blurred gaze followed the direction of her mistress's accusing finger.

"Will you take everything out of the trunk, please, and place the articles on this chair, one by one," commanded Mrs. Belknap.

The girl obeyed in stupefied silence.

"Do these articles—this fraternity badge, these hat pins, and this handkerchief belong to you, Jane?"

"No!—oh, my God, *no*!" cried Jane, staring with a suddenly blanching face at the little group of articles which Mrs. Belknap had singled out from among the things on the chair.

There was a tense silence in the room for the space of a minute; then Master Belknap's little feet were heard laboriously climbing the stair. "Muzzer!" he shouted, "I want 'oo, muzzer! I tan't find my Jane!"

Jane sobbed aloud.

"Oh, Jane, I *am* so *sorry*!" sighed Mrs. Belknap faintly. "Of course, you will have to go. But I shall not—" She hesitated over the harsh word, and finally substituted another. "I shall not tell anyone of this; except," she added firmly, "Mr. Belknap and Mr. Everett. I *must* tell them, of course. They will be sorry, too."

Jane stared at her mistress through a blur of anguished tears.

"Do you think—oh, you *can't* believe I did it?"

"What else *can* I believe?" Mrs. Belknap said sorrowfully. Then she arose with decision. "If you will come to me when you have packed, Jane, I will pay you your wages. And I do hope, my poor girl, that this will be a lesson to you. *Nothing* is so well worth while as truthfulness and honesty. *Try* to remember it, Jane, after this; will you?"

Jane's face hardened. "I didn't do it," she said doggedly. "That wicked Mary has been in my room. She said she had. She must have put these things in my trunk. I never saw them before."

"*Jane!*" exclaimed Mrs. Belknap; there was stern reproof, righteous anger, and a rapidly growing disgust in her voice. Then she swept out, pausing merely to say: "You may pack your things *at once*!"

John Everett came home early from the city that night. He had arrived at an important decision—namely, to make a confidante of his sister with regard to his unmistakable feelings for Jane. "Margaret is a brick!" he told himself hopefully. "She will understand; I know she will, and do the square thing by us both. It isn't as though Jane was a common, uneducated person; she is a lady to the tips of her little fingers—bless her!"

Mr. Everett's ideas had undergone a rapid and wonderful change within the few weeks of his meager acquaintance with Jane. He no longer appeared to himself to be breasting an unfriendly current of life with the mere vision of a distant, sunny shore to cheer his untiring efforts. He seemed suddenly to have attained a larger and completer knowledge of himself and of his powers. He knew himself to be abundantly able to make a home for the dearest, sweetest little girl in the world, and he was ready to ride rough shod and triumphant over difficulties of every conceivable sort. Since he had arrived at this by no means tardy conclusion of the matter, his love for Jane had over-leapt its barriers, and was ready to sweep all before it, including the girl's own delightful shyness and maiden coldness.

Mr. Everett found his sister Margaret at her little desk, a leather-covered account book open before her, a pile of bills and silver pushed to one side. He stooped to pinch her pink ear, following the pinch with a hearty brotherly kiss. Then he perceived that something was seriously amiss with the little lady. There were tears in her eyes and a piteous quaver in her voice as she looked up to greet him.

"What's the matter, little woman?" he asked gayly. "Won't the accounts balance?"

He bent nearer and read: "Jane Evelyn Aubrey-Blythe. Began work April 26th; wages $14.00."

"Is *that* her name?" he almost shouted. "Why didn't you tell me before?"

"I don't know what you mean, Jack," Mrs. Belknap replied petulantly. Then she burst into nervous tears as she faltered: "Jane's—*gone*! And, oh, Jack, she *wouldn't* take her wages!"

CHAPTER XIX

"Gone!" echoed John Everett blankly. "Are you telling me that Jane has *gone?*" Then he stooped over his sister with something almost threatening in his face and attitude. "Margaret," he said quietly, "you must tell me at once what has happened to Jane!"

Mrs. Belknap glanced up at him fearfully. "O Jack!" she cried, "surely you do not—you cannot——"

"How long has she been gone?" demanded her brother, still in that ominously quiet tone. "Tell me quick!"

"Not ten minutes," replied his sister. "But, Jack, *dear* Jack, listen to me! She—she—wasn't honest; I found——"

A smothered exclamation of wrath and grief, a loud slam of the front door, and the sound of his hurrying feet without reduced Mrs. Belknap to despairing tears.

"Oh! what shall I do?" she asked herself miserably. "I *tried* to be fair to Jane; I did indeed! I should never have accused her. But what *could* I think? And if Jack—oh! that would be worst of all! But perhaps he is just sorry for her; he is always being sorry for people. I wish she had taken the money; the sight of it makes me feel like a thief! And I wish—oh, I *wish* Jimmy would come!"

The little pile of bills and silver, representing the month's wages which she had urged upon poor Jane, seemed to accuse her solemnly. She put it hastily out of sight, glad of her child's insistent demands for attention.

The boy climbed upon her knee and pillowed his head comfortably upon her breast. "Jane cwied, muzzer," he remarked presently.

"Yes, dear," said Mrs. Belknap nervously. "Would you like mother to tell you about the three little pigs?"

"Uh-huh; tell me 'bout 'e' free 'ittle pigs. Jane cwied, muzzer!"

"Yes, dear. Now listen: Once upon a time there was a nice, kind pig mamma, and she had three dear, little——"

"Muzzer, if I—if I div Jane my fwannel el'phunt, would she—would she 'top cwi'in? I like my Jane, muzzer!"

"Poor little sweetheart!" exclaimed Mrs. Belknap, with a gratifying sense of indignation against Jane welling up warm within her. "Never mind about Jane, darling; listen to mother while she tells you about the three dear little

- 121 -

pigs. One was a little white pig, with pink eyes and a pink nose and the cunningest little curly tail."

"Was his 'ittle curly tail *pink*, muzzer?"

"Yes, dear; it was all *pink*, and——"

"*No!*" objected her son strongly; "his 'ittle curly tail was—it was— *Tell* me, muzzer!"

"It was—pinky white, a delicate, peach blossom sort of color," hazarded Mrs. Belknap. "Now be quiet, dear, and listen. The second little pig was spotted, white and——"

"If I div Jane my *wed bwocks*, would she 'top cwi'in, muzzer?"

"White and brown," went on his mother desperately. "Now you *must* listen, Buster, or mother cannot tell you the story. The third little pig was black—*all pure black*."

"Was his 'ittle curly tail all bwack, muzzer?"

"Yes; his little curly tail and all—*pure black*. He was the smallest pig of all; but his mother loved him dearly."

"Did he cwi, muzzer?"

"No; never; none of them ever cried. They were——"

"Jane cwied, muzzer."

"They were very good, obedient little pigs. They never interrupted their dear mother when she told them stories. They were——"

"I like my Jane," murmured the infant, applying his fists to his eyes, "an'—an' I like my supper. Tell Jane to div me my supper, muzzer!"

"Why, you poor little darling! Of course you must be hungry! Mother will give you your supper right away. Come, dear!"

Mrs. Belknap arose with a sigh of relief, and made her way to the kitchen. "Mary," she began, "I will give Buster his supper now; you may—" She stopped short in horrified dismay. Miss MacGrotty was lolling against the table, a saucepan grasped negligently in one hand, while its contents drizzled slowly down the broad expanse of her aproned front into a puddle on the floor.

"Why, *Mary!*" cried her mistress, "you are spilling that gravy all over yourself; do be careful!"

"*Careful*—is ut? *Careful!* I'm that—hic careful, mum! You'll not find me equal—on Shtaten Island, mum. I'm—jist a-ristin' mesilf a bit. I'm that wore out wid—hic—shlavin' fer the loikes av yez. An' I'll do ut no longer!"

Miss MacGrotty here relinquished her lax hold upon the saucepan which glissaded briskly to the floor, scattering blobs of brown sauce in every direction.

"*Mary!*" repeated Mrs. Belknap, "you must be ill!"

"Git out av me kitchen!" advised Miss MacGrotty trenchantly. "I'll not have the loikes av yez a-bossin' *me*! I'm a perfec' leddy, I am, an'—hic—I'll not put up wid yer lip no more, ner I won't put up wid hers neither—a-tellin' me I ain't honest, an' me on'y takin' me perquisites now an' thin in tay an' sugar an' the loike!"

"I do believe you've been drinking!" exclaimed Mrs. Belknap, a great light breaking in upon her mind. "Tell me, was it you who put those things in poor Jane's trunk?"

"Indade, an' I'll not tak' a worrd av yer imperance!" retorted Miss MacGrotty, with drunken dignity. "I says to mesilf, 'I'll tak' down her high looks,' I says. An' I done ut!"

Mrs. Belknap turned and fled—straight into the arms of her husband, who had just entered the house. In that safe refuge the little woman burst into tormented tears, while the infant clinging to her skirts lifted up his voice in sympathetic concert.

"What in the world?" began the distracted husband and father. "Hold hard here! I've got oranges, Buster! and violets, Madge! Come, dear, brace up and tell a fellow what's up! Anybody sick or dead? Or what has happened?"

Thus entreated Mrs. Belknap sobbed out an incoherent account of the untoward happenings of the day.

Mr. Belknap whistled, after a safe masculine habit. "Well, you have had a day of it!" he exclaimed. "Jane convicted and evicted; Jack eloped (presumably) and Mary intoxicated! By Jove! I believe she's preparing to invade the front of the house. Here, dear, you take the boy and go in the other room, and I'll manage the hilarious lady."

The rumble of a deep Irish voice and the slamming of furniture in the dining room presaged the dramatic advent of Miss MacGrotty, armed with a poker and a toasting fork. "I'll tak' down the high looks av her afore I'm done wid her!" she was declaiming.

"Hello, Mary! What's the matter with you?" demanded Mr. Belknap in a loud and cheerful voice.

At sight of her master, tall, broad and authoritative, Miss MacGrotty sank into a chair and began to weep hysterically. "Aw, sur!" she faltered, "may the saints in hiven bless your kind hearrt fur askin'! I've be'n that—hic—put upon this day, an' me a perfec' leddy, but that delicut an' ailin' I'm 'bliged to tak' a wee drap occasional to kape up me spirits loike! 'You've be'n drinkin'' she says. The imperance av her!"

Mr. Belknap had grasped the lady firmly by the arm. "You need a little rest, Mary," he said sympathetically. "You must have been working too steadily. My wife's a hard mistress."

"That she is, sur, bliss yer kind hearrt! If you'd lave me be, sur, I'd—hic—tak' down the high looks av her, an' that hussy, Jane, too. But I got good an' even wid *hur*!"

"What did you do to Jane?" inquired her captor, who was gently shoving his prize up the stairs.

"Don't you know, sur? an' you that shmart in your business? *She's* 'asy fooled! Sure, an' I changed things about a bit in the house; that's all I done."

"Ah-ha! Very clever of you, Mary. You put the missis's things in Jane's room—eh? Good joke that!"

Miss MacGrotty laughed hysterically. "She ain't found 'em all yit," she whispered. "Tell her to look between the mattresses av the bed."

"Thanks for the information, old girl!" observed Mr. Belknap genially. And having arrived at his destination, namely, the apartment occupied by Miss MacGrotty, he gently deposited his charge within; then shut and locked the door upon her.

"She'll sleep it off before morning," he told his wife reassuringly; "then I'll see that she leaves the house peaceably. I told you she was a fraud, dear. But never mind, better luck next time. As for Jack, I do hope he'll find that poor girl for the sake of the family peace of mind."

"I—I hope so too, Jimmy; only——"

"Don't worry about Jack," advised her husband. "He's too level-headed to rush into matrimony merely because he's sorry to see a girl treated unjustly."

"But, Jimmy dear," protested his wife, "I don't see what I could have done. There were the things—in her trunk."

Mr. Belknap shook his head. "It's pretty hard on a little woman when she's suddenly called upon to act as prosecuting lawyer, judge, jury and all," he said sympathetically. "But I think you were a bit hasty, dear. You might have suspended judgment, as they say, considering the defendant's general character."

"Yes, I really ought to have known better, I suppose," agreed Mrs. Belknap meekly. "But I can't help being afraid that Jack is more than sorry for Jane. And, Jimmy, she's *only a servant*—even if she is honest, and yes—I will acknowledge it—pretty."

"Talk about our glorious American democracy!" groaned her husband in mock dismay.

"Well, I'll put it straight to you, Jimmy Belknap; would *you* like Jane Evelyn Aubrey-Blythe for a sister-in-law?"

"Hum! That depends," said Jimmy Belknap, with a conservative grin. "But I say, Margaret, let's see what we can do about that dinner I seem to smell burning on the range."

While these important events were transpiring in the Belknap household, Mr. John Everett was having divers and sundry experiences of his own. As he plunged down the street in the fast-gathering darkness of the spring night he was conscious of but one desire, and that was to find Jane. Having found her, he knew definitely that he meant never to lose sight of her again. This much was certain, and the fine, drizzling rain which presently began to fall did not serve to dampen his resolution.

There was no car in sight when he reached the corner—no car and no waiting figure. One nearly always waited to the worn limits of one's patience on this particular corner, as Mr. Everett already knew from frequent experience. Traffic was light in this modest, detached suburb, and the traveling public correspondingly meek and long-suffering. But occasionally one did "catch" a car, despite the infrequency of the phenomenon. If Jane had gone—actually gone away into the great, wide, cruel world, how could he ever find her? And not to find Jane meant an aching desolation of spirit which already gripped him by the throat and forced the salt drops to his eyes.

"I *will* find her!" said John Everett to himself; and then, all at once, he found her.

She was standing under the sparse shelter of a newly leaved tree, her eyes shining big and tearless in the cold, white light of the shuddering arc-light.

"Jane!" cried John Everett. "Thank God I have found you, Jane!"

The girl looked up at him quietly. She did not reply; but the sight of his agitated face seemed to stir some frozen current of life within her. She sighed; then colored painfully over all her fair face. "She has told you," she said, "and you——"

"I love you, Jane," he said impetuously. "I want you to be my wife. O Jane dear, dear girl, don't turn away from me!"

"The car is coming," she said faintly. "You must not—oh, good-by, good-by!"

The brightly lighted car groaned and squeaked painfully to a standstill, and he helped her to mount the high step.

"Good-by," she murmured again; but when she looked up he was still at her side, feeling mechanically in his pocket for fares. "You must not go with me," she said firmly. "People will see you, and—and—I should prefer to be alone."

John Everett set his square American jaw. "I am sorry," he said briefly, "but I am going to see you to a place of safety somewhere. And to-morrow——"

"I do not need you," she said pointedly. "I am going to my friend, Miss Forbes, in New York."

"Very well," he agreed, "I will see you to your friend's house."

She did not once look at him till they had found places in a secluded corner on the ferryboat deck. Then she spoke again.

"I wish," she said gently, "that you would leave me."

John Everett looked down at her. "Jane," he said abruptly, "are you already married?"

"Why—why, no," she stammered. "Of course not!"

"Do you love another man?"

"No. But"—haughtily—"you have no right to ask me."

"I beg your pardon, Jane, but I have. Remember that I have asked you to be my wife."

"I am," said Jane, coldly and incisively, "a perfect stranger to you. At present I am a disgraced servant, leaving my place because I am accused of being—*a thief*."

"Jane, look at me!"

She obeyed him proudly.

"You are the woman I love, dear. I have loved you ever since I saw you that first day. I shall never love anyone else in the whole world. Oh, my poor darling, *don't* turn away from me; *try* to love me a little!"

In point of fact, Jane did not offer to turn away from him. Her bruised and lonely heart was filled with sweetest joy and light. And the proud little face uplifted to his was transfigured with the light that never shone on sea or land.

"Won't you try, dear?" he repeated, bending toward her.

"I can never forget," she said slowly, "that you loved me—when—" her tender voice broke piteously—"when all the world despised me."

CHAPTER XX

John Everett may, or may not, have been excusable for neglecting to inform Jane Blythe of a matter which nearly concerned her, and which had occupied his own attention for an hour or more that very day. The firm of lawyers with whom he was associated—Messrs. Longstreet and Biddle, to be exact—had received by the morning's post a letter from certain London solicitors instructing them to advertise for, and otherwise endeavor to locate the whereabouts of one Jane Evelyn Aubrey-Blythe, who was known to have left England for America on or about April 6th of the current year. Information regarding this person, who was otherwise described as being young and of pleasing appearance and address, would be thankfully received by Messrs. Thorn, Nagle & Noyes, attorneys and counselors-at-law.

In pursuance of this desired end, John Everett had been deputed to frame a suitable inquiry to be inserted in the public prints, and the leading New York, Brooklyn, and Jersey City papers were presumably at that moment setting the type for said notices. Just why Mrs. Belknap had neglected to inform her brother of what she had been pleased to term Jane's romantic but imaginary appellation, she could not afterwards recall.

It was Bertha Forbes who finally brought John Everett's soaring thoughts to earth again, when he presented himself at her lodgings as the escort of Jane on that memorable rainy evening in May. Miss Forbes was officially crisp and cogent in her manner at first; but thawed perceptibly when the two took her wholly into their confidence.

Jane had appeared quite unmoved by the news of the legal inquiry which concerned itself so particularly with her person.

"It will be Uncle Robert," she said calmly. "I suppose he has been frightfully annoyed at my disappearance—and Aunt Agatha, too. But," she added, with a fleeting glance at her lover, "I'm glad I ran away."

"So am I!" echoed John Everett fervently.

Bertha Forbes caught herself smiling. "Such foolish escapades frequently turn out quite otherwise," she said severely. "The question—now that this young person has been 'found,' so to speak—is what do Messrs. Thorn, Nagle & Noyes want with her?"

"They wish me to return to England—to Aunt Agatha," Jane was positive.

"You'll not go, Jane," whispered John Everett.

Bertha Forbes caught the whisper. "She may be obliged to go," she said curtly. "You must leave her for the present, young man, in my care. Communicate with your London lawyers and find out the particulars. Your plans for Jane's future are so extremely recent that they will bear deferring a bit, I fancy."

When John Everett went away at last, after bidding his sweetheart good night under the coldly impersonal eyes of Miss Forbes, he walked on air. And for exactly six days thereafter he was the happiest man on earth. On the seventh day arrived a cablegram from Messrs. Thorn, Nagle & Noyes, which read as follows: "Return Aubrey-Blythe next steamer. Sole heir to uncle's estate."

Jane shook her head when she heard this.

"Impossible," she said at first. "I have no uncle except Uncle Robert." Later she recalled the dim memory of a younger brother, one Foxhall Aubrey-Blythe, a wild scapegrace of a fellow, who had been bred to the army, sent to South Africa in the Zulu wars, and lost sight of by his family. "It was thought," she said soberly, "that he was killed, though his death was never reported in the despatches. He was officially starred and labeled 'missing'."

"He has evidently turned up again," said John Everett gloomily. "That is to say, he has been heard of again as rich and dead; and you are his heiress."

"It may not be much," said Jane Blythe thoughtfully. "I suppose," she added, "that I must go back to England. But I shall not stay there."

Then she looked at John Everett. He was staring sternly at the toe of his boot, a most unhappy expression clouding his handsome face. "You—don't like it—John?" she faltered, with an adorable little quaver in her clear voice.

He avoided her eyes. "I—ought not to have spoken to you as I did that night," he said at last. "Jane, I don't know what you will think of me. I—knew that the inquiry had been set on foot when I rushed out after you. I meant to have told you—*that*. But when I saw you—" He paused to groan aloud, then went on hurriedly: "I forgot all about that confounded letter from Thorn, Nagle & Noyes; I forgot everything except that I had found you. I was so sorry for you, dear, and so angry with my sister, and—well, I've come to the conclusion that I made a confounded fool of myself, Jane. Can you—can you forgive me?"

Jane's happy face had paled during this halting monologue. "I'm afraid I don't—understand," she said in a low voice. "Do you—mean that you are sorry you—told me——"

"I ought to have waited," he said doggedly.

"And if you had—waited?" she asked breathlessly.

He raised his unhappy eyes to hers. "If you had gone back to England free and rich you would have been glad to forget America and all your unhappy experiences here; wouldn't you, Jane? Why, when I think that I have actually sat still and allowed you to hand me my coffee of a morning I—I hate myself!"

"I hope," said English Jane tranquilly, "that I shall be allowed to hand you your coffee a great many mornings. Every morning, in fact, after we—." A great wave of lovely color rolled gloriously over her fair face. "O John!" she whispered, "didn't you mean it when you told me that you loved me?"

"Didn't I *mean* it?" he echoed. "Well, I should say I did!" And he looked it, to her complete satisfaction. "But——"

"You loved me when all the world despised me," murmured Jane. "I shall never forget that. Besides," she added shyly, "I—love you, and it would break my heart to——"

"Darling!" exclaimed John Everett. "Then we'll be married to-morrow. For to tell you the truth, Jane, I'm downright afraid to let you go back to England alone."

Of course this ridiculously hasty decision of John Everett's had to be severely modified and reconstructed by the various ladies nearly concerned in the case. Bertha Forbes, for one, immediately took a hand in the affair and pooh-poohed the notion of such unseemly haste.

"What do you know about this young man, anyhow, that you should be willing to marry him out of hand in this mad fashion?" she demanded with decided acrimony.

"I love him," Jane replied, with stubborn tranquillity. "I shall never love anyone else," she added confidently.

"What about Mr. Towle?" inquired Bertha coolly.

"Mr. Towle!" echoed Jane, with an air of extreme surprise. "What, pray, has Mr. Towle to do with it?"

"Isn't he a lover of yours?"

"I'm sure I can't help *that*," pouted Jane, with a shrug of her slim shoulders. "He is ages older than I am, and besides——"

"Well," grunted Miss Forbes, "go on; what other crimes has he committed?"

"Of course he can't help being bald, poor man. But, Bertha, he came to see me one day at Mrs. Belknap's; I can never forgive him for that. Fancy his waiting in the kitchen, and being sent away—like a—like a butcher's boy! But that wasn't enough, even; he came back and persisted in talking to me on the kitchen porch. Do you know if it hadn't been for Buster interrupting, just as he did, I actually believe I should have—that is, I *might* have—and only think, Bertha, how *horrible* that would have been! No; he shouldn't have come. I shall always think so."

Miss Forbes stared meditatively at the girl for a long minute; then she burst into what Jane was disposed to regard as unreasoning laughter of the variety which was once sapiently characterized as "the crackling of thorns under a pot."

"I can't see," observed Jane, very grave and dignified, "why you should laugh. There was nothing to laugh about in what I said."

Miss Forbes instantly grew sober. "Heaven forfend that you should ever see, my dear child," she observed in a grandmotherly tone, "and far be it from me to attempt an explanation! Suppose we talk about clothes, instead. And—how will you ever go to work to metamorphose that late imperious mistress of yours into a fond sister-in-law?"

But Mrs. Belknap came to the front full of tears and handsome apologies and congratulations, all mixed up with embarrassed blushes and smiles, and wouldn't dear Jane forgive her, and in token thereof be married from her house?

Jane was inclined to be a trifle stiff with her prospective sister-in-law at first. Recent memories were far too poignant to admit of the new relationship with real cordiality. But she relented perceptibly when Master Belknap flung himself upon her with glad cries of joy.

"I yuve my Jane!" he cooed confidentially. "I'm doin' to div' oo my fwannel el'phunt an'—an' my wed bwocks, if 'oo won't cwi any more, Jane."

"You must call her Aunt Jane now, Buster," observed his uncle, who was watching the scene with an air of proud proprietorship.

"I yuve my Aunt Jane," amended the infant docilely. Then, eyeing his male relative with a searching gaze, "Have you dot any choc'late dwops, Uncle Jack?"

Jane laughed outright at this.

"You'll come; won't you, dear Jane?" pleaded Mrs. Belknap, seizing the auspicious moment.

"I'm afraid Mary MacGrotty would——"

"She's gone, thank Heaven!" exclaimed Mrs. Belknap with a shudder. "I haven't a soul in the house."

"And I can't cook, you know," murmured Jane teasingly, as she hid her blushing face on the infant's small shoulders.

"Don't rub it in, Jane," advised Mr. Belknap urgently. "We'll have a caterer and everything shipshape. Later, though, when you're back from England you'll do well to let Madge here give you some cooking lessons. Buster and I would have starved to death long ago if we hadn't been able to keep our cook; wouldn't we, old fellow?" And he tossed his son and heir high above his head amid a burst of infant exuberance.

And so it was finally settled. The excellent Bertha Forbes handed over her official duties to an underling for a whole week, while she shopped and sewed and fetched and carried for Jane with an untiring devotion, which earned that small person's lasting gratitude and friendship. On the day of the simple home wedding Miss Forbes stood up, tall and grenadier-like, bearing the bride's bouquet, with so uncompromising an air and manner that Master Belknap actually desisted from three several pieces of mischief while he gazed solemnly at her with large, round eyes.

When the last flutter of pearl-gray veil and white handkerchief had faded from view on the deck of the retreating steamer, Miss Forbes wiped her eyes openly. "I'm glad she's gone," she said sternly. "She ought never to have come."

"If Miss Jane Aubrey-Blythe had not entered this port with five thousand dollars of lace upon her person, she would not now be leaving it under such happy auspices," observed Mr. Belknap mildly. "And that, Miss Forbes, would be on the whole, a regrettable circumstance; don't you agree with me?"

"Hum!" said Bertha Forbes, rather shamefacedly, "I bought in some of that very lace at a customhouse sale. It was that which trimmed her wedding dress. I thought"—firmly—"that it was no more than right."

Mr. Belknap cast an admiring glance at the lady. "Miss Forbes," he said feelingly, "your sense of poetic justice does you credit; it does indeed. I hope we shall see a lot of you in the future. Our house on Staten Island is always open to you."

"Thanks," said Bertha Forbes gruffly. But she shook hands with right manly heartiness when she took leave of the little party on the dock, and she actually kissed the infant, while depositing an unwholesomely large box of confectionery in the pocket of his coat. "It is a shame to call this child *Buster*," said Miss Forbes. "I detest the name myself; think it exerts a positively demoralizing influence on the character. *I* shall call him Everett in future."

And she did so on the numerous pleasant occasions when she visited the Belknap family.

As for Master Everett, thus happily restored to his rightful appellation, he actually came to adore Miss Forbes, and called her his "dear old Berfa," to her immense delight and satisfaction.

CHAPTER XXI

One morning two weeks later as Lady Agatha Aubrey-Blythe, her daughter Gwendolen, and her two sons Percy and Cecil were gathered rather aimlessly in Lady Agatha's private morning-room, "a lady" was announced, as desirous of speaking with Lady Agatha.

"Who is it, Susan?" asked Lady Agatha of the maid, who appeared all of a tremble with some carefully suppressed excitement.

"Oh, my lady, it's Miss Jane Evelyn as ever was!" declared Susan, beaming with doubtful delight.

"*It's Jane!*" exclaimed the group in concert.

"Show her up at once, Susan," said Lady Agatha, with a graciousness which allayed poor Susan's fears. "Children," she added, turning to her attentive offspring, "you must remember that our dear Jane is quite an heiress now."

Gwendolen put up a haughty lip. "I don't want her here, even if she is," she said disagreeably.

"Of course you don't!" crowed Percy. "Jane's a beauty and you aren't!"

"Percy—*my son!*" exclaimed Lady Agatha warningly, and swept forward to greet the small, slight, bright-eyed person who entered the room escorted by the broadly smiling Susan.

"My *dear* Jane!" murmured Lady Agatha, enfolding the little figure in her voluminous embrace. "How we *have* suffered since your cruel desertion of us!"

"I suppose it must have annoyed you, Aunt Agatha," said Jane sweetly. "But it couldn't be helped, you see."

Then she turned to the two boys, who had greeted her vociferously, and to Gwendolen, who sulkily offered a cheek to be kissed.

The girl's bright eyes were misty and she trembled a little as she looked from one to the other. English sights and sounds and faces had never seemed so delightful, yet she was no less determined upon leaving them all for the land of her adoption.

"How much money did Uncle Foxhall leave me?" she asked, after the buzz of greetings and questions had somewhat subsided.

"Why, don't you know, my dear?" Lady Agatha exclaimed. "I thought the solicitors would have told you before this. It is not a large sum; but it will serve to alter your future materially. It is a trifle short of twelve thousand pounds, I believe; but with *that* at your back I shall be able to arrange a very suitable marriage for you, I am sure. In fact, I have already mentioned quite an eligible *parti* to your uncle, a Mr. Gildersleeve. He is a widower of excellent family, my dear Jane, and *quite* suitable in every respect."

"He's an old frump," put in Gwendolen, with a hateful little laugh, "but I dare say he'll do for *Jane*."

"My *dear* Gwendolen!" protested Lady Agatha. "Of course, now that you can afford to dress in a manner becoming to your station, Jane, I shall not mind taking you out with Gwendolen—at least, *occasionally*. By the way, that is a very pretty frock you are wearing. Where did you get it, my dear?"

"This is an American gown," said Jane, drawing up her little figure with a proud smile, "and this," she added tremulously, "is an American—ring."

"*What!—a wedding ring!* You are not *married already?*"

"Yes," said Jane, with a blush that made her look handsomer than ever. "My husband is waiting for me downstairs. I should like you to meet him, Aunt Agatha, and you"—including the others with her smiling glance. "He is an American," she finished, with a touch of hauteur which was not lost on Lady Agatha, "and we sail for—home a week from to-day."

Being doubly assured of this desirable *dénouement*, Lady Agatha actually went to the length of giving a family dinner party in honor of her niece by marriage, and to this dubious merry-making the Hon. Wippingler Towle was bidden by the express commands of the master of the house.

"You've clean thrown away a good lump of money, Towle," grumbled Mr. Aubrey-Blythe; "but perhaps it will afford you some satisfaction to look at the hole."

"I shall certainly be glad of the opportunity to meet—er—Mrs. Everett once more," Mr. Towle said politely. "But I—er—don't quite follow you in your remark about the money." His stern eyes actually threatened his friend. "I am told that your niece has lately inherited a small legacy by the bequest of—er—a deceased relative, which will, I trust, make her quite comfortable and happy in her new home."

"Damn it, Towle!" blustered Mr. Robert Aubrey-Blythe, in the language of the hunting field; "I can't follow your lead, sir; I'd come a damned cropper, if I tried."

"Don't try, then," advised Mr. Towle curtly.

Being duly presented to the bride and to the groom, who comported himself on the happy occasion with an ease and composure which Lady Agatha

Aubrey-Blythe later characterized as "brazen American boldness," Mr. Towle shook hands with both, with such a singular and unpleasant mist clouding his glass that he was immediately thereafter obliged to resort to a vigorous and prolonged use of his large, scented cambric handkerchief. And this circumstance spared him the knowledge of Jane's smiling coldness of manner.

Later in the evening Mr. Towle found himself unable to resist the opportunity of a *tête-à-tête* which Gwendolen's half sneering, half curious appropriation of the young American made possible. Jane was seated upon a sofa engaged in a wholly hollow and perfunctory conversation with Lady Agatha, when Mr. Towle tentatively approached. Lady Agatha instantly made room for him with an air of undisguised relief which brought a faint smile to Jane's lips.

When she looked up to greet her late elderly suitor she was still smiling, and the circumstance gave him courage to say, rather stiffly: "I have not as yet—er—spoken with you upon the subject of your marriage, Mrs.—ah—Everett; I trust you will permit me to wish you all happiness, and—er——"

"Thank you, Mr. Towle," said Jane sweetly.

She had already acquired, he reflected, the self-possessed air of the young matron, and her clear eyes were gazing at him with a shade of retrospection in their depths. She was thinking—and the man was unhappily aware of the fact—"what if I had married you!"

She sighed gently and stole a glance at her young husband, who was smiling with open amusement at Gwendolen's clumsy attempts to make game of him. "I fear," she said kindly, "that I was very rude to you the last time I saw you. But I——"

He waited for her to go on.

"I was really very unhappy, and when one is unhappy——"

Again she paused to glance at the young American whose handsome, vigorous head stood out in bold relief against the crimson cushions of his chair. "When one is unhappy it is difficult to—to be just to others. I have talked it all over with my—with Mr. Everett since our marriage, and he says you were a brick—*a brick*; yes, I am quite sure that is what he called you; but it really means something very nice and—square. You see words in America frequently mean something far different from what one has always supposed; and I am learning as fast as I can. But my husband says that I did not appreciate how awfully kind it was of you to come to America just to look for me. You did come for that; didn't you?"

"I had," said Mr. Towle gravely, "no other motive in going to America."

"Well, that being the case," Jane went on rapidly, "it wasn't a bit nice of *me* to send you away without a word of explanation; now was it? But this is the real, true reason; I don't mind telling it now." She paused to smile happily to herself—"I caught a glimpse of Mr. Everett coming up the street, and—and I thought it would be very awkward for you—for him—to meet just then. I hope you are not too horribly vexed with me?" She smiled brilliantly upon him, with an obvious desire to be at peace with all her little world.

"Hum—ah," began Mr. Towle, eyeing the wistful little face which was inclined toward his with a sternness born of his determination not to make a fool of himself. "I—I beg to assure you, Mrs. Everett, that I—er—quite understand, and I am not disposed to——"

Jane's eyes drooped; so did the corners of her mouth. "I never seem able to say the right thing at the right time," she said mournfully. "I see that I have offended you again, and I only meant to tell you—to apologize for——"

"Jane," said Mr. Towle, in the deep, caressing tone which Jane had heard only twice before from his lips, "I forgive you for—everything, and I hope you will believe me when I tell you that I hope for nothing better in life than to hear that all is going well with you, and that you are—happy."

"Thank you," said Jane softly. Her eyes beamed kindly upon him. "You are very good," she said; "I think I shall be even happier because you have said this."

And the Hon. Wipplinger Towle in his own peculiarly patient, middle-aged fashion blessed her in his heart of hearts for that little word "even." It was, in a way, one of those crumbs which sometimes fall from a rich man's table, and as such he thankfully appropriated it as his own meager share of the loaf which an unfriendly Fate had denied him.

THE END